DANGEROU[S]

'They're not coming,' said Tracy. 'I told
you Mark wasn't involved. Didn't I
tell you?'

'Shh!' said Belinda.

'I won't shush,' said Tracy. 'I'm telling
you – '

'I think I heard something,' interrupted
Belinda.

They sat poised in absolute silence,
hardly daring to breathe. A few
suspenseful seconds ticked by.

'What do you think you heard?'
asked Holly.

'A car,' whispered Belinda. She doused
the candle. The sudden darkness sent
shivers down their spines.

'Oh, lordy . . .' murmured Tracy.

They all heard it. The sound of
footsteps on the front porch. Holly crept
on all fours to the head of the stairs
and slid an eye round the banisters.
Her breath hissed as she saw a shadow
through the glass panels in the front door.

'It's them,' she whispered. 'Belinda, get
to the phone. Quick!'

The Mystery Club series

Dangerous Tricks
The Mystery Club 5

Fiona Kelly

KNIGHT BOOKS

Hodder and Stoughton

Printed and bound in Great Britain for Hodder and Stoughton Children's Books, a division of Hodder and Stoughton Ltd, Mill Road, Dunton Green, Sevenoaks, Kent TN13 2YA (Editorial Office: 47 Bedford Square, London WC1B 3DP) by Cox & Wyman Ltd, Reading, Berks. Typeset by Hewer Text Composition Services, Edinburgh.

A Catalogue record for this book is available from the British Library

ISBN 0 340 59283 4

1 Tracy's new friend

'You don't think Tracy's been kidnapped, do you?' said Belinda.

'I wouldn't have thought so,' said Holly. She looked at her watch. 'She's only fifteen minutes late.'

It was a bright afternoon in the small Yorkshire town of Willow Dale. Holly Adams and her friend Belinda Hayes were standing on a corner. Opposite them, the multiplex cinema dominated the far side of the street. They were in the more modern outskirts of the town, far removed from its peaceful, unchanging centre.

They were waiting for Tracy Foster, the third member of the Mystery Club.

'I'm not hanging about here much longer,' said Belinda. 'Where's that girl got to?' She peered up and down the street from behind her wire-framed spectacles. She had a round face and straggly mouse-brown hair that fell over a forehead that was, at the moment, wrinkled with annoyance.

'We'll give her another five minutes,' said Holly.

1

She was taller than her friend, slim and brown haired, with intelligent grey eyes.

'OK, but if she's not here by then, I'm off home,' threatened Belinda. 'I'm half-starved already.' She looked around for somewhere to sit down and, finding nothing, leaned heavily against the wall. 'I'm tired out,' she said.

'You're always tired,' said Holly. 'Anyway, you can't go home. We've been talking about visiting the library for an entire week now. Don't you want us to find something for the festival?'

The day of the annual Willow Dale Festival was approaching. It was to be Holly's first festival – her family had only been in Willow Dale for a few months – and she wanted to be properly involved in the festivities. Which was why she had suggested to her friends that they go to the library in search of information about old local customs. Holly thought they should come up with something different for the school to do this year.

'She's probably been waylaid by Kurt,' said Belinda. 'You know what those two are like when they get together.' Kurt Welford was Tracy's occasional boyfriend. Belinda thought boys were a waste of space. Holly didn't mind Kurt one way or the other – except when he made Tracy late.

'She's more likely to be showing everyone that report I did in the school magazine of her winning

2

the tennis tournament,' said Holly. 'She said it was the best bit of writing I've done.'

'Only because it was about *her*,' said Belinda.

As soon as she had arrived at the Winifred Bowen-Davies school, Holly had headed straight for the editor of *Winformation*, the school magazine, hoping to become their star reporter. She had been slightly offended by being given hockey matches and suchlike to review, but at least it had meant she was involved.

It was also through an advertisement Holly had placed in the magazine that the Mystery Club had been formed. The idea had been to set up the club to help Holly make new friends. She had hoped to find lots of people who shared her interest in mystery novels. In the event, only Belinda and Tracy had turned up. Tracy, because she felt it was her duty to join every club in the school, and Belinda because her mother had nagged her to a shadow about joining in more. And, as Belinda said, 'I shall read one of those mystery books of yours one day.' But up to now real life had proved even more exciting than Holly's beloved mystery novels.

Not that they searched for strange goings-on. Things just seemed to happen to them, and the three girls had got themselves involved in some extraordinary adventures in the few months since Holly and her family had moved from London.

3

'Look!' said Holly. 'There she is.' Tracy and a boy had come out of a side road.

'And she's with Kurt,' said Belinda. 'What did I tell you?'

'That's not Kurt,' said Holly. 'You need new glasses.'

It certainly wasn't Kurt, as even Belinda could see now she looked properly. The boy with Tracy had black hair and Kurt's hair was blonde. And he was shorter than Kurt, and thinner, with a narrow, sharp face.

'Who is it, then?'

'I don't know. Oh – yes I do. It's that new boy. What's his name? He's in the year above us. Mark something. I know: Mark Greenaway.'

'Him?' said Belinda, rolling her eyes. 'Trust Tracy.'

'What's that supposed to mean?' asked Holly. 'You don't even know him.' The Greenaways had been in Willow Dale for only a few weeks.

'His parents are absolutely potty,' said Belinda. 'Haven't you heard? My mum got it all through the local grapevine. She was telling me all about it the other evening.' Belinda's mother was a leading light in Willow Dale society, and it was important to her that she knew everything that was going on.

'Your mum is the world's worst gossip,' said Holly. 'I like to think I'm above that sort of thing.' Tracy caught sight of them and waved.

4

Holly waved back. 'Quickly,' said Holly. 'Tell me *all* about it before they get here.'

'His mother is some sort of whacky faith healer,' Belinda began. 'And his father is a kind of magician or something. They've taken the lease on a shop in Radnor Street. Apparently they – oh, hello, Tracy. You're late.'

Tracy came bounding along the pavement, her blonde hair bouncing on her shoulders and her blue eyes sparkling. Mark Greenaway followed in her energetic wake.

'Hi, you guys. I want you to meet Mark,' said Tracy, her American accent more obvious than usual. She always sounded more American when she was excited. Her father was American, but since the divorce three years ago, she had been living in Yorkshire with her English mother, who ran a nursery. 'Mark, this is Holly. You two should have lots in common – Holly's from London, too. Mark's folks have just moved up from London, Holly.'

'The place must be almost empty,' said Belinda. 'Have they got the plague down there or something?'

'This is Belinda,' Tracy told Mark. 'Don't worry about her – she's always like this. These are my absolute best friends, Mark. You wouldn't believe the things we've gotten involved in since Holly showed up.'

5

'Tracy tells me you've set up a mystery club,' Mark said with a smile. 'It sounds interesting.'

'Interesting is hardly the word,' said Belinda.

'We do seem to get tangled up in some strange things,' said Holly. 'Only the other week – '

'Mark used to edit a school magazine in London,' interrupted Tracy. 'I've suggested he has a word with Steffie – perhaps he could write some stuff for our mag.' Steffie Smith was the editor of the school magazine. 'He could start up a magic column. You know loads of magic tricks, don't you, Mark?'

'A few,' said Mark. 'My parents perform at parties and things like that. I know a few simple tricks.'

'Don't be so modest,' said Tracy. 'Mark's got this great trick with a watch, haven't you, Mark? Go on – show them.'

'OK,' said Mark. 'If someone will lend me a wristwatch.'

'Don't look at me,' said Belinda. 'My watch cost a fortune. My mum would kill me if anything happened to it.'

Holly unclasped her wristwatch and handed it to Mark. 'What part of London are you from?' she asked.

'We had a place in Kensington,' said Mark, taking out a handkerchief and wrapping it round Holly's watch.

'Whereabouts in Kensington?' asked Holly. 'I

might know it. We used to go shopping around there sometimes.'

'You wouldn't know it,' said Mark. 'It was just a little street round the back of Harrods. But then my parents decided they'd had enough of the rat race, so we ended up here. What brought you here?'

'My mum was offered managership of her own branch of the bank she works for,' said Holly. 'My dad was a solicitor, but he'd been wanting to give it up to concentrate on his carpentry work for ages – so Mum's transfer seemed the perfect opportunity. I felt a bit out of it to start off with, but this is a lovely place once you get used to it and make a few friends.'

'It's a bit dead, though, isn't it?' said Mark. 'Still, I suppose I'd better try and make the best of it. If my parents make a go of their shop we'll probably be stuck here for a while.'

'What do they sell?' asked Holly, preferring to ignore his uncomplimentary remarks about the town that she had grown to love.

'Oh – magic tricks, herbal remedies. Wholefood. You know – new age stuff. All sorts of things. You ought to take a look.'

'I can't wait,' Belinda said drily. 'We are really short of magic tricks and wholefood in this town.'

Mark laid the bundled handkerchief on the pavement. 'OK,' he said. 'Stand back while I say the magic words.'

They stepped backwards. Mark stretched his hands out. 'Hocus pocus, never fear – let the wrist-watch disappear,' he said solemnly. He looked round at them. 'That's it,' he said. 'It's gone.'

They looked down at the folded-up handkerchief.

'I bet it was never in there,' said Belinda. 'You've probably tucked it up your sleeve.'

'Search me if you like,' said Mark.

Holly bent to pick up the handkerchief.

'Just a second,' said Mark. He lifted his foot and stamped down heavily on the handkerchief. There was a disturbing crunching noise. Holly's jaw fell open.

'Oh, dear,' said Mark. 'It doesn't sound like it worked, does it?'

'My watch!' yelled Holly.

Mark crouched and gingerly unwrapped the handkerchief. Broken bits of watch were revealed. He looked up at Holly. 'I'm really sorry,' he said. 'It *usually* works.'

Holly was speechless.

Mark picked the handkerchief up. 'I'll pay for it. How much did it cost?'

'I don't know,' said Holly, aghast. 'My brother Jamie bought it for me for Christmas last year.'

Mark pulled a fat wallet out of his back pocket. 'I'll pay for a new one,' he said. 'It's the least I can do.'

'But it was a *present*,' said Holly. 'You can't just

buy a new one as if . . . ' She stopped. Mark had opened the bulging wallet and had pulled out a wristwatch, holding it by the strap between finger and thumb.

Tracy burst out laughing.

'Will this one do instead?' asked Mark, waving the watch in front of Holly's eyes. It was her own wristwatch. Undamaged.

Belinda grinned. 'He had you going with that one, didn't he?' she said. 'I told you your watch was never in there. Not a bad trick. Not bad at all.'

Holly examined the watch. It was hers all right. 'How did you do that?' she asked.

'Magic,' said Mark.

Holly strapped her watch on, trying to join in with the general amusement, but feeling slightly annoyed that she had been taken in by his trick.

'Didn't I tell you he knows some good stuff?' said Tracy. 'Wasn't that great?'

'Very clever,' said Holly, frowning at Mark. 'You won't catch me out like *that* again.' Her face cleared. 'OK,' she said. 'It was good. You had me fooled.'

'He's got loads of other tricks,' said Tracy.

'The library will be closing in half an hour,' said Belinda. 'If we're still going there.'

'Hey, listen,' said Tracy. 'Do you guys mind if I take a rain-check on that? Mark's invited me to the cinema. Why don't we all go see

9

a movie instead? We can visit the library any old time.'

'I think I'll give it a miss,' said Holly. 'We keep putting the library off, and the festival is only two weeks away. If we don't think of something soon it'll be too late.'

'Oh, OK,' said Tracy. 'You two have a good time, then. I'll tell you all about the film tomorrow. Coming, Mark?'

They crossed the road, leaving Belinda and Holly gazing after them.

'Well,' said Belinda. 'She didn't waste any time. I wonder what Kurt will make of that?'

'She's just being friendly,' said Holly. 'You know what she's like. I expect he feels like I did when I first arrived. She's just taking him under her wing. It's a bit odd, though, him saying he lived in Kensington.'

'What's so odd about that?' asked Belinda. 'People do live there, don't they?'

'Yes, but he said they lived in a street round the back of Harrods. Harrods isn't in Kensington. It's in Knightsbridge, and it's an incredibly posh area. They'd have to be really rich to live somewhere like that.'

'Perhaps they are,' said Belinda.

'What? With a magician dad and a mother who does faith healing?' said Holly. 'I wouldn't have thought so.'

'Perhaps his dad's a really *famous* magician,' said Belinda. 'Or maybe Mark just made it up to try and impress us. Does it matter?'

'I suppose not,' said Holy. 'It's a bit odd, that's all. And I didn't like that comment he made about Willow Dale being dead.'

'He's only just got here,' said Belinda. 'Give him a chance.'

They headed towards the library.

'I think I saw how that trick was done,' said Belinda. 'Lend me your watch and I'll give it a try.'

'Not in a million years,' said Holly. 'I don't want your great hoof coming down on it. I nearly had a heart attack with Mark just then, and he knew what he was doing.'

The library was a modern building, part of the rash of newer houses and offices and shops that had been built round the quiet, old heart of the town. Inside, they went straight over to the desk with the computerised filing system. Belinda sat down, and started tapping the keyboard.

'Now, then,' said Belinda. 'What shall we look under?'

'F for folklore?' suggested Holly.

The visual display screen quickly filled with green writing. 'Got it,' said Belinda. 'Right. Follow me.'

They gathered half a dozen heavy books from the shelves and took them over to the reading tables.

'This is perfect,' said Holly, as they started going through the books. 'There's lots of stuff here. We're bound to be able to come up with something.'

As they pored over the books Holly couldn't help overhearing a couple of women chatting at the next table. She didn't *listen*, but her natural inquisitiveness made it impossible for them not to gain her attention.

'That's two burglaries in the past fortnight,' said one of them. 'It's getting so you don't feel safe in your own home.'

'I know,' said the other. 'And they say that the burglars knew exactly what to take.'

'Well, I'm having window locks fitted,' said the first one. 'I know I haven't got a house full of antiques like they do over in Fitzwilliam Street – but you can't be too careful.'

'Did you hear that?' whispered Holly. 'Fitzwilliam Street – that's only round the corner from you.'

'I know all about it,' said Belinda. 'Mum's going round checking all the doors and windows every night. They'd have a field day in our place. Unless they went into my room, of course. Still, you never know. Perhaps they'd steal all those horrible expensive clothes my mum keeps trying to get me to wear. I wouldn't mind *that*.'

Despite her wealthy background, Belinda insisted on slopping around in jeans and an old green sweat-shirt. Her only concession was her thoroughbred horse, which to her mother's despair, she had named Meltdown.

'Anyway,' said Belinda. 'Don't start trying to solve these burglaries. I've had more than enough excitement with you recently. Let's concentrate on finding something interesting for the festival, shall we?'

'I've got it,' said Holly. 'Look at this.'

She pointed to the open book. There was a column of writing and a drawing of a woman decked out in a huge, colourful costume and mask. '"The Carnival Queen,"' read Belinda over Holly's shoulder. '"In olden days a young girl from the local community was chosen to be queen of the carnival. She was led through the streets decked out in flowers, accompanied by a jester, and followed by other members of the community dressed as animals. They passed in procession through the streets of the town, and the carnival reached its climax in a sacred grove, where a bonfire was lit and where the revellers spent the night feasting and carousing."' Belinda looked round at Holly. 'I don't remember anything like that at our festivals before,' she said. 'It sounds like we could have a lot of fun with that.'

'We could have a carnival queen, couldn't we?' said Holly brightly. 'We could make the costumes at school. That would be brilliant. What do you think?'

13

'It sounds promising,' said Belinda. 'The school always has its own float in the procession. If we could convince them to do it as a carnival queen float it would be the best thing the school's done for years.'

'And my dad could help build the float,' said Holly. 'He's great at things like that. Do you think Tracy would be interested in joining in?'

'Interested?' said Belinda. 'She'll want to be the carnival queen if I know her. I can just see her in that costume.'

'We can take this idea to the school festival committee at the next meeting,' said Holly. 'The carnival queen will have to be chosen by the entire committee, but it wouldn't do any harm to suggest Tracy. She'd love it, wouldn't she? Standing up on a float in a fancy costume. Waving at everyone and being the centre of attention.' She gave Belinda a mischievous grin. 'Unless you fancy doing it, of course?'

'Very funny,' said Belinda. 'I'd rather die first. But I'll recommend you as the jester, if you like.'

'No thanks,' said Holly. 'I don't fancy performing. I'd rather just help out with putting the whole thing together.'

'Well, that's it, then, isn't it?' said Belinda. 'We'll tell Tracy all about it in the morning.' She put her hand to her ear. 'I can hear something,' she said. 'There's a tub of chocolate chip ice cream in the freezer at home – it's calling out for me to go and eat it. Coming?'

'You bet!' exclaimed Holly.

They caught the bus over to the better part of town, where Belinda lived with her mother and father in their huge chalet-style house.

They were sitting eating ice cream at the kitchen table when Belinda's mother came in. She looked briefly in a mirror and patted her immaculate hair.

'Hello, Holly,' she said in her usual brisk way. 'Are you looking forward to our party?'

'What party?' asked Holly, looking at her friend.

'I forgot to mention it,' Belinda said glumly. 'Dad's going away to work in Brussels for a month. We're having a going-away party.' She gave a hollow grin. 'It'll be such fun.'

'It *will* be,' said her mother. She smiled at Holly. 'Anyone would think I was planning a trip to the dentist,' she said. 'I've told Belinda she can invite all her friends. And I've arranged a surprise.'

Belinda gave her a worried look. 'What sort of surprise?'

'You'll find out,' said her mother, sailing out of the room.

Belinda shook her head. 'I hope it *is* a surprise,' she said. 'Knowing my mother, it's more likely to be a shock.'

'Don't be such a misery,' said Holly. 'It might be fun.'

Belinda looked hollowly at her. 'It'll be dreadful,' she said. 'Take my word for it. It'll be absolutely dreadful.'

2 Tracy vanishes

Holly made her way across the lawn to the shed that housed her father's workshop. Carpentry tools hung in neat, precise rows from hooks on the walls, or lay on the long workbench ready for use. Various items in stages of completion filled most of the floor space.

Mr Adams was bent over the humming lathe, skilfully shaving strips from the length of wood that spun beneath his chisel.

Holly stood silently watching him work for a few minutes, as the rough chunk of wood was transformed into a smooth, perfectly-shaped chair leg.

Her father sat back, pulling his goggles down to dangle round his neck, and switching the lathe off. He looked round at her, smiling.

'I've got to have a set of six dining chairs ready for Tuesday fortnight,' he said with a grin.

'Who are they for?' asked Holly.

'A big house up near where Belinda lives,' said Mr Adams.

'I heard a couple of women talking about burglaries over there,' said Holly.

Her father nodded. 'I read about it in the *Express*.' The *Willow Dale Express* was their local newspaper, run by the father of Tracy's friend Kurt. 'We'll have to be extra careful that everything is kept locked up,' Mr Adams said. 'We don't want someone coming in and thieving all your books, do we?' Holly's mystery novels occupied an alcove-full of shelves in her bedroom.

'How long do you think it will take you to finish the chairs?' Holly asked innocently.

'No more than a week.' Her father looked at her with a bright gleam in his eyes. 'Why?'

'Oh, no reason. I just wondered.'

Mr Adams laughed. 'You never *just* wonder anything. What have you got planned for me?'

'You're so suspicious, Dad.'

'Not without reason. Come on, out with it.'

Holly told him about the coming festival and the ideas she and Belinda had for a carnival queen float.

'And you thought maybe your kind and helpful dad might be able to do some work on the float,' he said. 'Is that it?'

Holly smiled hopefully. 'Could you?'

'Of course. What needs doing?'

'It hasn't been decided yet. Belinda and I are going to take our ideas to the festival committee meeting at school.'

Mr Adams nodded. 'Get back to me when you've come up with some concrete ideas.' He pulled his goggles back up over his eyes. 'And now you'd better leave me to get on with these chairs, or I shan't have time to do anything for you.'

Holly gave him an affectionate hug.

'Thanks, Dad. If they know we've got expert help they're bound to agree with our plans.'

She went into the house and up to her bedroom, looking forward to the committee meeting the following morning.

Tracy had, of course, wanted to be on the committee, and she had been quite put out to discover the first meeting coincided with her violin practice.

Belinda and Holly didn't have a chance to speak to her before break the next morning.

'We'll tell her all about it once it's been decided,' said Belinda, as they made their way to the room where the committee meeting was being held. She sighed. 'I can invite her to the party at the same time.'

'You don't sound like you're looking forward to that party,' said Holly.

'Oh, I've got nothing against having a few friends round, by my mum is bound to invite all *her* lot, and they'll bring their kids as well.' She looked darkly at Holly. 'There's bound to be masses of little kids there, and some of her friends have got the most

19

horrible children you can imagine. And I'm still not happy about this surprise she's got planned.'

There were already half a dozen or so people in the room. One of them was Steffie Smith, the editor of the school magazine. Holly and Steffie had been rubbing each other up the wrong way since they had first met. Steffie was fiercely protective of the way she ran the magazine, and habitually ignored Holly's occasional suggestions for changes.

Miss Baker, who was running the committee, was sitting on a table, swinging her legs and waiting for everyone to arrive.

She held her hands up for silence. 'OK,' she said. 'You've all had time to think about the school float, so let's hear what you've come up with.'

Various ideas were debated. Someone suggested a Chinese fire-breathing dragon. Someone else thought of a pageant of schools down the ages. There was a lot of shouting and disagreeing until Holly explained the carnival queen idea.

'That sounds more like it,' said Miss Baker. 'I can see some potential in that.'

Holly expanded on her idea. 'We could dress up in Middle Ages costumes. We could even have minstrels.'

'We'll need a carnival queen,' said Miss Baker. 'Anyone fancy that?'

'I nominate Tracy Foster,' said Holly. 'She'd make a great queen.' There was another long debate. They still hadn't come to a decision when the bell went for the end of break.

'That's all we've got time for now,' said Miss Baker. 'We'll meet again tomorrow morning to sort out who's doing what. There's lots to do and only a fortnight to do it in, so you'd all better be ready to give up a fair bit of your spare time.'

At lunch-time, Holly and Belinda went to look for Tracy. They met Kurt coming out of the canteen.

'Seen Tracy?' asked Belinda.

'Yes,' said Kurt, stepping sideways to pass them and walking rapidly down the stairs.

Holly hung over the banisters. 'Where?' It wasn't normal for Kurt to be so abrupt with them.

'She's gone off somewhere with that new boy,' said Kurt without looking round. He vanished round the bend of the staircase.

'Oops,' said Belinda softly. 'Someone's nose has been put out of joint. Do you think she realises that she's upset him? Perhaps we should say something to her?'

'Best *not*,' said Holly. 'You know what Tracy's like if she thinks people are telling her what to do.'

Holly and Belinda finally managed to track Tracy down. She was sitting on a low wall by the care-taker's sheds. She was with Mark Greenaway and they were surrounded by a small group.

Holly stretched over the heads of the circle of

21

people. Mark had three playing-cards laid face-down on the wall.

'That one!' said Tracy, pointing to the left-hand card.

Mark picked it up. It was a Queen.

'Easy,' said Tracy.

'You've got very sharp eyes,' said Mark. 'How about we have a little bet? I bet you ten pence you don't get it this time.'

'You're on,' said Tracy.

Holly stepped in closer as Mark moved the three cards on the wall. 'There you go,' said Mark. 'Where's the Queen?'

'There!' said Tracy, pointing to the middle one. 'No problem.'

Mark lifted the card. It was the three of clubs. Tracy groaned and the small crowd laughed.

'Want to try again?' said Mark. 'Win your money back?'

'No way,' said Tracy. 'You're too good for me.' She looked up and spotted her friends. 'Did you see that?' she said. 'Is he quick, or what?'

'Do you want to hear about the festival meeting?' asked Belinda, giving Mark a disapproving look. 'Or are you too busy throwing your money away?'

Tracy moved away from the crowd. Someone else sat opposite Mark to try his luck.

Holly told Tracy about the carnival queen idea. Tracy's eyes lit up.

'I knew you'd go for it,' said Belinda. 'Prancing about on the float in a big costume, waving at the adoring crowds.'

'Is it going to be videotaped, like last year?' asked Tracy. 'I could make a copy to send my dad.'

'Has the school got the facilities to video the festival?' asked Holly. 'I didn't know that.'

'The parents clubbed together and bought a camcorder last year,' said Belinda.

'I hope they let me do the videoing,' said Holly. 'I think I'd be good at it.'

'Don't get your hopes up,' said Belinda. 'Your pal Steffie did it last year.'

Belinda told Tracy about the party at her house.

'Have you invited Mark?' asked Tracy.

'Not as such,' said Belinda, with a knowing glance to Holly. 'But he's welcome to come along if he wants to. I thought you might like to ask Kurt.'

'Oh. OK,' said Tracy. 'If I see him.' She looked over her shoulder to where Mark was entertaining the small crowd with his card tricks. 'I'm sure Mark would enjoy it,' she said. 'It will make him feel more at home – more like one of us. I'll go and have a word with him about it.'

They watched as she pushed her way back through Mark's audience.

'Well?' said Belinda to Holly. 'Kurt *and* Mark? This party might turn out to be more interesting than I was expecting.'

Belinda wasn't happy. All her darkest forebodings were coming true. Her mother had filled the house with her society friends and their masses of children. She had even got in a catering firm to provide a buffet. And Belinda had been bludgeoned into wearing a party dress.

Small groups of adults stood around, chatting about mortgages and savings accounts and fretting about the recent spate of burglaries. Swarms of little children ran in and out of the rooms and up and down the stairs.

Belinda's friends were in a corner, keeping out of the way. Holly, Kurt, Tracy and Mark.

Kurt was being very quiet. Holly had tried to bring him into the conversation by mentioning to Mark that he took photographs for the local newspaper. But Mark had steam-rollered him into silence with a long monologue about all the photos *he* had taken when he was in London.

Holly was beginning to find Mark's one-upmanship a bit irritating. It seemed that no matter what you mentioned, Mark had done it – and had done it better than anyone else.

The one thing that Mark seemed impressed and surprised by was the size of Belinda's house.

'You don't look like someone who comes from a place like this,' he said.

'Don't I?' said Belinda. 'So how should I look?'

'If I had all this money I'd come to school in a chauffeur-driven Rolls Royce,' said Mark. 'I'd show off a bit.'

Belinda gave him a polite smile. 'I'll mention it to my dad,' she said frostily. 'He's always looking for ways of throwing money away.'

'You could ride to school on Meltdown,' said Tracy with a laugh. Mark looked puzzled until Tracy explained about Belinda's horse.

'You've got a *horse*?' he said. 'What on earth for?' He looked round at the others. 'What's the point of having a horse?'

Belinda shot him an expressive look but didn't say anything. Horses were Belinda's first love, and no one got away with insulting them.

'I wonder when your mother's surprise is due,' said Holly, changing the subject to avoid an argument.

Mark looked at his watch. 'In about ten minutes,' he said.

Belinda frowned at him. 'How do you know that?'

Tracy grinned. 'It's a secret,' she said. 'You'll see.'

'Seeing that everyone except me seems to know what's going on around here,' said Belinda, 'I think

25

I'll go and get something to eat.' She pushed her way to the long table with the impressive buffet. Holly followed her, noticing that Kurt had drifted off to stand on his own.

'I've gone right off that Mark,' said Belinda, filling her plate. '"What's the point in having a horse?" What a stupid thing to say. I've never come across anyone as bigheaded as him in my entire life. And pretending he knows what my mother has cooked up. Talk about conceited!'

'Tracy seemed to know something as well,' said Holly. 'Maybe your mother told her, and she told him. But you're right; he does seem to be a bit of a show-off. Did you notice the way he didn't let Kurt get a word in?'

'I'm surprised Tracy likes him,' said Belinda. 'I thought she had more sense.'

Just then Mrs Hayes's voice rose above the general hubbub.

'If you'd all like to come through into the drawing-room, we've got some entertainment for you.'

'This is it,' said Belinda. 'The dreaded surprise.'

The drawing-room was at the back of the house. It was long and elegant, with heavy curtains covering the French windows that led down into the Hayeses' enormous garden. Furniture had been moved to the edges of the room and rows of chairs had been set up.

26

Tracy was waiting at the door. There was no sign of Mark.

'Let's sit at the front,' said Tracy. 'We'll see everything better from there.'

In a clear space in front of the curtains stood a small laden table, and on the floor was a large black box, like a trunk. On the front of the box, in gold letters, was written 'The Great Mysterioso'.

'It's a magic show,' said Holly, sitting between Belinda and Tracy.

The audience settled down. Someone switched the lights off.

There was a loud bang, a flash of light and a gush of red smoke. A tall man stood centre-stage, dressed all in black with a large cloak and slicked-down black hair.

'Good evening, ladies, gentlemen and children,' roared the Great Mysterioso. 'And welcome to my cavalcade of enchantment. Allow me first to introduce my assistant, Marybelle the Clown.'

A figure dressed as a clown came running down from the back of the room and took a bow. Holly could tell that it was a woman, despite the make-up. She wore baggy red polka-dot trousers and rainbow-coloured braces. Her face was covered by a rubber clown mask and there was a shock of ginger hair spraying up from a wig on her head.

'It's Mark's mom,' whispered Tracy.

'How do you know?' asked Belinda.

27

'The Great Mysterioso is Mark's dad,' replied Tracy. 'Mark told me all about it. Shush and watch.'

The show began. The Great Mysterioso pulled swathes of coloured flags out of the clown's mouth. He made bottles appear and disappear from under handkerchieves. The clown juggled red balls then threw them to the Great Mysterioso. The balls vanished in the magician's hands and then reappeared in unexpected places.

Against her better judgement, even Belinda ended up having to admit that he was very good.

'And now,' declared the Great Mysterioso, 'for the grand finale we will need a brave volunteer from the audience.'

The clown jumped forwards and grabbed Tracy's arm.

'Aha,' said the Great Mysterioso. 'A willing volunteer.' He rubbed his hands together and grinned fiendishly at the audience. 'And what's your name, young lady?'

'Tracy,' she said, giving Holly and Belinda a grin.

The Great Mysterioso opened the lid of the black box. 'Would you be so kind as to step inside my magic box, Tracy?' he said.

Tracy climbed into the box and crouched down. The Great Mysterioso closed the lid on her and fitted a padlock to the front.

He stood behind the box. 'And now,' he said, 'before your very eyes, Tracy will vanish from the box.' There was another blinding flash and a plume of red smoke. The box looked exactly the same.

'The key, if you please,' said the Great Mysterioso, holding his hand out to the clown.

The clown felt in her pockets. She put her hand over her mouth. 'I've forgotten it,' she said.

'What?' said the magician. 'You've forgotten the key? How are we to show everyone that Tracy has disappeared?' He shook his head at the audience. 'You just can't get good assistants these days.'

He stepped out in front of the box. 'Surely someone here will have a key that fits the lock.' He ran his eyes along the front row and pointed at Belinda.

'You, young lady,' he said, taking Belinda's arm and drawing her out of her seat. 'You look the sort of person who might have a key to fit the magic box.'

'I don't think so,' said Belinda.

'Do you have *any* keys on you?'

'Well, yes . . . in my bag, but . . . '

'May I see them?'

Belinda picked her bag up from the floor and handed the magician her keys. He went through them, choosing a key and taking it off the ring.

'This is the one,' he said.

'That's my front door key,' said Belinda.

'We'll see,' said the Great Mysterioso. He handed the key to her. 'Try it in the padlock.'

Belinda leaned over the box. The key fitted into the lock.

'Oh!' She gasped as the padlock fell open. 'It fits.'

'Stand back,' said the magician. He lifted the lid of the box. The front fell open.

It was empty.

Tracy had vanished!

3   A question of faith

'She's behind the box!' Belinda shouted through the applause that greeted Tracy's disappearance.

The Great Mysterioso swirled his cloak, leaned to unclip some hidden catch, and stepped back as the entire box collapsed in on itself.

'Wrong!' cried Holly, clapping along with the rest of the audience.

The Great Mysterioso took the key from Belinda and looped it back on to her key-ring.

Belinda frowned for a moment then laughed as the magician returned her keys to her with a deep bow. 'She's behind the curtain,' she said.

'I see we have a true sceptic amongst us,' said the Great Mysterioso. He looked out over the heads of the crowd. 'Will Marybelle the Clown come forwards, please,' he called.

Holly looked round. She hadn't noticed that the clown was missing. She came down from the back of the room.

'Open the curtain and reveal who is hidden there,' said the magician.

31

Marybelle pulled the curtain aside. A small, slim, blonde-haired woman stepped forwards from behind the curtain. Belinda blinked, her mouth hanging open.

'May I introduce my wife, Mary,' said the magician. 'And may I also reveal the face behind Marybelle the Clown.'

Marybelle pulled her mask off. It was Tracy. She waved and grinned.

The three of them linked hands and bowed to renewed applause and yells of delight.

Belinda sat down, clapping along with the others as the three performers swept out of the room.

Mrs Hayes stood up and waved the audience to silence. 'If the children would like to stay here, I've arranged for some party games,' she said. 'And for the rest of us, there's music. So come on, everyone, let's do some dancing.'

Music started up from another room and the adults began to file out.

'Well?' said Holly to Belinda. 'Explain that away.'

'OK,' said Belinda, 'I'll admit it. I don't know how they did the switch. But I *do* know how they did the bit with the key. The key he handed me to open the padlock wasn't my door key at all. It was very slick, but he must have palmed my one.'

'How do you know that?' asked Holly.

Belinda grinned. 'Because mine has my initials scratched on it. And the one he handed me didn't.'

She showed Holly her key-ring. 'See? I didn't let on I'd noticed because I didn't want to spoil his trick.' Sure enough, the letters 'BH' were scratched on the grip.

Belinda stood up. 'Anyway,' she said, 'if everyone's going to be dancing, that'll mean the buffet table will be deserted. I think I'll go and get another plateful. Coming?'

They found Kurt on his own by the table.

'Enjoying it?' asked Holly.

Kurt shrugged. 'Tracy seems very taken with that Mark Greenaway,' he said. 'I haven't had a chance to speak to her all evening.'

Holly gave him a sympathetic look.

'Speak of the devil,' murmured Belinda. Mark came into the room with a big grin on his face.

'Pretty impressive, wasn't it?' he said. 'Of course, I know how it's all done. I can do all those tricks standing on my head. It's simple once you know.'

'Is there anything you can't do?' asked Kurt.

'Not much,' Mark said smoothly. 'Seen Tracy?'

'Not recently,' said Belinda.

'She's probably waiting for me to dance with her,' said Mark. He walked to the door, glancing over his shoulder and smiling at Kurt. 'I'm a brilliant dancer. You can come and watch, if you want to pick up some tips.'

Kurt waited until he was gone, then put his plate down. 'I'd better be getting off home,' he said.

'Don't go yet,' said Belinda.

'I've got some work to do,' said Kurt. He gave them a bleak smile. 'Thanks for inviting me. Say goodbye to Tracy for me. I don't want to disturb her.'

'I'm going to have a word with that girl,' said Belinda after they had seen Kurt to the door. In the other room they saw Tracy dancing with Mark.

'Are they *glued* together, or what?' said Belinda after waiting to try and get Tracy on her own. When she and Mark weren't dancing, they were chatting together.

'Let's leave it,' said Holly. 'We can talk to her tomorrow. And when we do, I want to find out how that disappearing trick was done. She must have been in on it from the start.'

'Don't count on her telling you,' said Belinda. 'It's probably a big *secret* between them.' She wriggled uncomfortably in her dress. 'Let's go and see if there's anything left to eat.'

'Come on, Tracy,' said Holly. 'You can tell us.'

They were in the classroom waiting for the next festival meeting to begin.

Tracy shook her head. 'I'm sworn to secrecy,' she said. 'I'm not allowed to tell anyone.'

'We're not just *anyone*,' said Belinda. 'We don't keep secrets from one another. It's not as if we're going to blab it all around the school.'

34

'OK,' said Tracy reluctantly. 'If it's that important to you, I'll tell you. But you mustn't let on to anyone that you know. Is it a deal?'

Holly and Belinda nodded.

'There's a panel in the back of the box,' said Tracy. 'While all that smoke was billowing about, I crawled out and got out through the French windows. Mark's mother had slipped out while no one was watching. She was waiting for me round at the front of the house. I got into her clown outfit while she crept back in through the French windows. It was as simple as that.'

'The French windows are kept bolted,' said Belinda. 'How did you manage to get them open without anyone spotting you?'

'We unbolted them in advance,' said Tracy. 'So all I had to do was push them open and slip out.'

'Did you notice that Kurt went early?' said Belinda.

'Did he?' said Tracy.

'He was a bit upset, I think,' said Holly.

'Upset about what?' asked Tracy.

'Can't you guess?' said Belinda.

'Now, look,' said Tracy. 'Kurt doesn't own me. I'm allowed to pick my own friends without asking his permission. Mark doesn't know anyone up here. I just want to help him feel at home.'

'Well, you're certainly doing that,' said Belinda.

Tracy frowned at her. 'What's that supposed to mean?'

But there was no chance for them to speak further as the other members of the festival committee began to come into the classroom.

Miss Baker came and sat on the table at the front. 'OK, everyone,' she said. 'Let's get some jobs allocated. I don't want us leaving here until everybody knows exactly what they're doing.'

It was a noisy, chaotic meeting, but by the end everyone had been given their tasks. Holly and Belinda had been put in charge of designing the float with the help of the woodwork and art departments, and Tracy had been chosen as carnival queen.

Tracy went up to Miss Baker at the end of the meeting. 'What will the queen actually be doing?' she asked. 'I've had an idea. I'm sure Mark Greenaway and his father would be able to think of some bits of magic that I could perform.'

Miss Baker nodded. 'Sounds good,' she said. 'Let me know what you come up with.'

Belinda confronted Tracy outside the classroom. 'What's all this about magic tricks? Holly and I came up with the idea of the queen. You're not planning on pulling rabbits out of hats, are you? That's not what we had in mind at all.'

'It'll be more interesting than just standing there waving,' said Tracy. 'I'm going to ask Mark if he'll help. Miss Baker thinks it's a good idea, even if you don't.'

'There is one trick I'd like to see him perform,' said Belinda. 'The vanishing Mark Greenaway trick. Permanently.'

Tracy frowned at her. 'I don't understand what you've got against him,' she said.

'Do you want a list?' asked Belinda. 'How about, he's a big-headed know-all, for starters?'

'OK,' said Tracy. 'I know he sounds a bit like that, but it's just because he's nervous. He talks like that to cover it up. You'll see. Once he gets to know you, he'll settle down and start behaving naturally. You've got to give him a chance, you guys.' She frowned at them. 'I'll see you later.'

They watched as she walked down the corridor.

'Do you believe that?' asked Belinda.

Holly shrugged. 'Maybe,' she said.

Belinda rolled her eyes. 'The guy's a creep,' she said. 'And he'll carry on being a creep whether Tracy believes it or not.'

Holly shrugged again. She hoped that Mark Greenaway wasn't going to cause a major rift between her two friends.

*   *   *

37

The following morning Mr Adams came to the breakfast table with the post, and with a leaflet that he had found on the doormat.

Holly's mother glanced at the leaflet. '"Mary Greenaway,"' she read. '"Faith Healer. Come and discover the power of faith to make you whole."' She laughed. 'She's having a public meeting tonight at Heron Hall.'

'What's a faith healer?' asked Jamie.

'A faith healer is someone who claims they can make people well without medicine,' said their mother. 'It's a load of old nonsense.'

'You don't think people can really be made better by faith healers, then?' said Holly, reading over her mother's shoulder.

'No, I don't,' said Mrs Adams. 'It's the biggest con there is. The likes of Mary Greenaway can't cure real illnesses.'

Holly took the leaflet to read.

'Her son Mark has just started at school,' said Holly. She went on to explain about Mark and his family. While Holly wasn't looking, Jamie grabbed the leaflet and began to fold it into an aeroplane.

'I was reading that, you pest,' said Holly, trying to grab the leaflet back.

'No fighting at the breakfast table,' said Mrs Adams. 'Jamie, give that back to your sister and go and get your school bag. You'll be late, the pair of you, if you don't hurry.'

38

When Holly got to school she found that a lot of the leaflets had been distributed in the town.

'She's a fraud,' declared Belinda. 'You can bet on it.'

'That's what my mum said,' agreed Holly. 'But I'd still be interested in seeing for myself.'

'I suppose we could go along for a laugh,' said Belinda. 'And to see how it's done. Have you got any ailments you'd like cured?'

'Only Jamie,' said Holly. 'But I don't think Mary Greenaway would be able to do much about him. Shall we see if Tracy wants to come?'

'I don't think that's such a good idea,' said Belinda. 'Not with her being so protective of Mark at the moment. She probably wouldn't approve of us going along to convince ourselves that his mother is a con-lady.'

'No,' said Holly. 'Perhaps you're right. We'd better go on our own.'

Heron Hall was part of a recent development of municipal buildings. It was capable of holding a couple of hundred people. By the time Holly and Belinda arrived that evening it was already more than half full.

'Do you think all of these people are believers?' Belinda whispered as they found themselves seats near the back. 'Or just nosy, like us?'

'It's difficult to tell,' said Holly, looking round. 'There are all sorts of people here.'

The stage was bare save for a microphone stand and a tall, solitary stool.

More people filed into the hall, and soon it was all but full.

'Surely they can't all be ill,' said Belinda.

Before Holly had the chance to reply, the main lights in the hall went down and a single spotlight came to rest on the stool in the middle of the stage.

Mary Greenaway walked slowly across the stage and perched on the stool.

'Welcome,' she said. 'My name is Mary Greenaway. Tonight you will witness remarkable things. Tonight you will see how disease and pain can be driven away by the power of faith. I claim no special abilities for myself. All I shall do is help you to discover your own inner powers.'

'What does she mean by inner powers?' whispered Belinda. 'Is she going to turn us into super heroes or something?'

'Shh!' hissed Holly. 'I'm trying to listen.'

Mary Greenaway stepped to the edge of the stage. She pointed down to the front row. 'You, madam,' she said. 'I can sense that there is pain within you. Would you come up and be healed?'

Everyone craned their necks as an elderly woman stood and shuffled up the steps at the side of the stage.

Mary Greenaway rested her hand on the woman's head. 'You suffer from many pains,' she said. 'Let your faith be joined with mine so that the pain is driven out.'

There was a breathless silence.

'Is the pain gone?' asked Mary Greenaway.

'Yes,' said the woman, sounding surprised and delighted. 'It's gone away completely.'

Mary Greenaway turned to the audience, her arms outstretched. 'You have witnessed the power of faith!' she declared.

'That's old Mrs Witherspoon from the charity shop,' whispered Belinda. 'I've known her for years. She's got a season ticket to the doctors'. She's a complete hypochondriac. You name it, and she's got it. I'm not convinced by *that*.'

A trickle of people began to make their way up to the stage to be touched by Mary Greenaway.

After a while she came to the edge of the stage. 'There is an unbeliever here,' she said. 'I can sense it.'

'She probably means you,' whispered Holly.

'A man,' said Mary Greenaway. 'A man with pain in his body.' She reached out her arms. 'Please. Come forward. Have faith.'

Nothing happened for a few moments, then a ripple went through the crowd as a man made his way to the aisle and hobbled up towards the stage. With painful slowness he mounted the steps. Mary

41

Greenaway moved over to help him, bringing him to the centre of the stage.

'I can help you,' she said. 'You have suffered the pain of arthritis for many years, haven't you?'

'That's right,' said the man. 'I've been to doctors all over the country, but none of them could help me.'

Mary Greenaway rested her hands on his head. 'You will be cured!'

Holly and Belinda watched in amazement as the man seemed to grow stronger and taller in front of their eyes. A smile broke out on his face.

'Do you believe in the power of faith?' cried Mary Greenaway.

'Yes!' said the man. 'Yes! I believe!'

'Your faith has cured you,' said Mary Greenaway. 'You will suffer no more.'

The man stretched his arms and legs. 'The pain has gone!' he said. He ran across the stage and bounded down the steps. 'I'm cured!' he shouted.

There were cries of astonishment from the audience, and a huge burst of applause. The faith healing meeting was over.

'Well?' said Holly. 'What did you make of that?'

Belinda shook her head. 'I don't know,' she said.

They made their way to the entrance. A couple of police officers were standing by the door.

'Could you all wait a moment,' shouted one of

them. The buzz of voices died down. 'Is there a Mrs Pomeroy here?'

A prosperous-looking middle-aged woman pushed her way to the front. 'I'm Mrs Pomeroy,' she said.

'Would you come with us,' said the police officer. 'I'm afraid we've got some bad news for you. Your house has been burgled.'

Holly and Belinda looked at each other as the crowd began to push forwards.

'She lives down the far end of my street,' breathed Belinda. 'These burglaries are getting closer all the time.'

4 Clues in the post

It was breakfast time at the Adams house. Jamie was scribbling some last minute homework. Mr Adams was looking at sketches that Holly and Belinda had made for the design of the school float.

Holly was giggling over a long letter from her friend Miranda. Miranda Hunt and Peter Hamilton had been two of Holly's closest friends when she had lived in London. Miranda and Holly wrote regularly to each other – and even Peter sent the occasional postcard. Half of Miranda's letter was taken up by a comic account of car-mad Peter getting himself doused with oil whilst doing something under his father's car.

Mrs Adams came in with a copy of the *Express*. 'It's all over the front page,' she said. 'How many burglaries does that make altogether? Four or five now, isn't it?' She looked at her husband. 'I'll feel better when you've fitted those window locks.'

'I'll do it today,' said Mr Adams. 'Don't worry.' He looked at Holly. 'They seem to be concentrating in your friend Belinda's part of the world.'

'I know,' said Holly. She glanced up at her mother. 'Does it say whether the police have got any leads?'

'It says a downstairs window was smashed and that the place was completely turned over,' said her mother. 'Apparently the police are puzzled because all the other burglaries up to now have been very neat in-and-out jobs without much damage.' She tossed the paper on to the table. 'I suppose the burglar saw that all the lights were off and just took a chance.'

'And poor Mrs Pomeroy was at the faith healing meeting all the time,' said Holly. 'That must have been a nasty shock for her.'

'It's a pity that Mary Greenaway isn't a clairvoyant as well as a faith healer,' said Mrs Adams. 'That way she'd have known what was going to happen.' She pulled on her suit jacket. 'And clairvoyants make more money than faith healers as well.'

'Mrs Greenaway doesn't ask people to pay,' said Holly.

Her mother smiled knowingly. 'Not at a public meeting she doesn't,' she said. 'That's just to get people hooked. Just you wait. She'll be having private consultations soon.' She headed for the door. 'And don't forget those window locks,' she called back.

'I shan't,' said Mr Adams. 'They'll be on by the time you get home.'

45

The front door slammed. Mr Adams looked at the sheet of designs again.

'Some of these are a bit adventurous,' he said. Holly and Belinda had come up with various ideas. One was to have the float done up like a ship. Another was to make it look like a castle, with Tracy perched on a turret. 'I really think you ought to go for something a bit more simple.'

'Like what?' asked Holly.

'A galactic battleship,' said Jamie. 'With flashing lasers and sonic cannons. You should get modern, Holly. Have Tracy dressed up as an alien invader. I could give you some ideas.'

'Thanks,' said Holly. 'But I think we can manage without your help.' She looked at her father. 'Have you got any ideas?'

'Well, yes, I have, actually,' he said. 'The theme is an ancient fertility custom, isn't it? All magic and mystery? I think you should do the float up to look like a magical wood. You could fix struts to the float and make trees out of hardboard. Some painted flowers to go with Tracy's flower costume, and there you are.'

'Boring,' said Jamie, rolling his eyes.

'No, it's not,' said Holly. She grinned at her father. 'I think that's a great idea. I can't wait to tell Belinda.'

*　　*　　*

46

'It's a brilliant idea,' said Belinda. 'Much better than the things we dreamed up. And your dad reckons we can get all that done in time?'

'Yes,' said Holy. 'He doesn't think there will be any problems at all. Hardboard tree-trunks. Paper leaves. A green canvas strip painted with flowers to go round the bottom of the float. The crafts department should be able to supply all of that. It'll be terrific.'

At lunch-time they went first to Mr Thwaites in the woodwork studio to give him their plans, and then on to the art department to show Mr Barnard what they had in mind for the decoration round the float's canvas skirt.

They were just heading for the canteen when Holly spotted Jamie, his hands deep in his pockets, a thunderous frown on his face.

'What's up with you?' she asked.

'Your stupid festival,' he said. 'I bet it was your idea, too.'

'What?' asked Holly.

'There's going to be a school stall, selling things for charity. A stall set up outside the Town Hall where the parade ends,' moaned Jamie. 'And I've been recruited to help make things for us to sell. I told them I was no good at that sort of thing. I even suggested we could have a charity football match instead, but they wouldn't listen.'

'What sort of things have you got to make?' asked Belinda.

'I don't know yet. I've got to go to a meeting after school. It'll be something stupid, I bet. They're going to show us how to use plaster of Paris.'

'Well, you can't blame me,' said Holly. 'It wasn't my idea. Anyway, it might be fun.'

'Perhaps they'll let you make plaster of Paris aliens,' suggested Belinda.

Jamie looked a bit brighter. 'Do you think so?' he said.

'It's worth asking,' said Holly.

Jamie went off, full of ideas for plaster monsters and spaceships.

'Have you seen Tracy today?' Holly asked as she and Belinda sat in the canteen.

'Briefly,' said Belinda. 'She was with Mark. Cooking up magic tricks for the festival, I expect.'

'Did you mention that we were at his mother's meeting last night?' asked Holly.

'I didn't get a chance to speak to her,' said Belinda.

'What did you make of it all, last night?' asked Holly. 'I've been thinking about it, but I can't make up my mind one way or the other. Do you think Mary Greenaway's genuine?'

'She seemed normal enough,' said Belinda. 'But I don't know if that means anything. I suppose I

48

was expecting it to be all flowing robes and weird incantations.' She shrugged. 'I don't know.' She took a thoughtful bite of her roll. 'You know,' she said, 'we could always take a look at that shop they've started up. Remember, I told you they'd taken over a shop? It's in Radnor Street. Do you know it?'

Holly shook her head.

'It's over in that oldie-worldie bit round by the church. You know, where they have all those antique shops,' said Belinda. 'I don't know which shop, exactly, but it wouldn't take us five minutes to find it. What do you say we have a look after school today?'

'OK,' said Holly. 'After all, if I'm going to be a journalist when I leave school, I'll be expected to investigate curious things like this, won't I? It'll be good practice.'

'That's right,' said Belinda. 'And just think, if we do manage to unmask her as a fraud she'll have to give all those people their aches and pains back.' She laughed.

Holly laughed as well. 'I don't think anyone will thank us for that,' she said. 'But I would like a look round that shop, all the same, whether we discover any dark secrets or not.'

The network of streets round the church was Holly's favourite part of Willow Dale. Completely unspoilt, it was like stepping back into Victorian times.

Holly and Belinda made their way down Radnor Street. The tall, narrow buildings were divided by dark alleys.

'This has got to be it,' said Belinda. They stood outside a small shop with its door sunk between two bottle-glass windows. A newly painted sign hung above the door, 'The Green Way.'

'Cute name,' said Belinda. 'The Green Way, run by the Greenaways. It's a good job their name wasn't Winterbottom.'

'I don't know,' said Holly. 'They could have sold thermal underwear if it was.'

There was a sign on the door:

Under New Management
Please Come In And Browse.

Holly peered through the windows. One side of the shop teemed with coloured bottles and jars and herbal remedies. The other was full of witch and monster masks and boxes containing magic tricks.

'It's just like the shop in that Charles Dickens novel,' she said. '*The Old Curiosity Shop*.'

'Stop showing off,' said Belinda. 'You know I haven't read any Dickens.'

Holly laughed. 'It was serialised on television. It was about this girl called Little Nell, who – '

50

'Don't start telling me the plot,' Belinda interrupted. 'I know you once you get into explaining things like that. We'll be here for hours. I'll wait for the re-runs.' She grinned at Holly. 'Well? Do we take the plunge?'

'Why not,' said Holly. 'It says we're welcome to browse.'

A bright bell chimed as Holly pushed the door open. The shop smelt strongly of incense and soft bubbly music played quietly in the background. The shop was filled with racks and shelves. There were Hallowe'en costumes and magic tricks, herbal remedies and thin paperback books on homeopathy and aromatherapy and strange subjects the girls had never heard of. A tall cabinet was filled with packets of beans and cereals.

At the far end of the shop was a long counter. Mary Greenaway was sitting behind it. She was reading, but she looked up as the two girls came in. There were no other customers.

'Can I help you?' she asked.

'Not at the moment, thanks,' said Belinda. 'We're just looking.'

There was certainly plenty to look at. Holly spotted some bubble-wrapped packs of tricks and games on a revolving rack.

'Jamie would love these,' she said. There were rubber spiders and trick soap that promised to make your face go black. There were very realistic-looking plastic chocolates and sugar cubes that dissolved in your tea to reveal horrible black flies. Everything, in fact, that a boy like Jamie could have hours of fun with.

'Don't tell him,' warned Belinda. 'It would be chaos if he got his hands on any of these.' She went over to a cabinet filled with jars of herbs.

'Take the lid off and have a smell,' said Mary Greenaway. 'Those herbs have a lot of different uses. Mixed together in the right proportions they can cure headaches and toothache and upset stomachs.'

'How do they do that?' asked Holly, sniffing at a jar that smelt strongly of aniseed.

'In the old days herbs and spices were the only medicines people could get,' said Mary Greenaway. 'There are natural remedies for every ailment. Cloves for toothache and peppermint for stomach pains. It's all there.' She smiled. 'I haven't needed to go to a doctor for years.'

'These things could cure anything, could they?' asked Belinda.

'Very nearly,' said Mary Greenaway.

'Even a broken leg?' asked Belinda.

Mary Greenaway's smile didn't falter. 'A broken leg isn't an illness,' she said.

'I don't know,' said Belinda. 'I broke my leg falling off my horse a couple of years ago and I felt pretty ill.'

Mary Greenaway leaned forward, her eyes sharp and bright. 'You're making fun of it,' she said. 'It's very easy to mock.'

'Sorry,' said Belinda. 'I didn't mean to sound rude.'

'It doesn't matter,' said Mary Greenaway. 'It's not easy these days to keep faith with the old ways.'

'We were at your meeting last night,' said Holly. 'You seemed to be able to cure those people without any herbs or anything.'

'Some of us are born with special gifts,' said Mary Greenaway.

'Can you cure really serious illnesses?' asked Holly.

'So long as the sufferer has faith,' said Mary Greenaway.

'And what if they don't have faith?' asked Belinda.

Mary Greenaway's smile faded. 'Without faith nothing is possible,' she said.

'I'm sorry,' said Belinda. 'But that sounds like a bit of a cop-out to me.'

'I beg your pardon?' said Mary Greenaway, the smile wiped clean away.

'Well,' said Belinda cautiously, 'it means you can never be proved wrong, doesn't it? Because if someone doesn't get better after seeing you, then you can just say they didn't have enough faith.'

'Many people have been relieved of their pain because of me,' said Mary Greenaway.

'Yes, but . . . ' began Belinda.

Mary Greenaway waved a hand. 'I'm not going to argue with you about it,' she said.

'I was only saying . . . '

Mary Greenaway stood up. 'Are you intending to buy anything?' she asked, her voice taking on an impatient edge. 'I'm going to be closing up in a few minutes.' She touched her fingers to her forehead. 'I have a headache,' she said. 'So if you're not going to buy anything . . . ' She smiled faintly and unconvincingly. 'Perhaps you could come back another time?'

A minute later the two girls stood on the pavement outside. They watched as the bolt was shut and the blind pulled down.

'Do you think I upset her?' asked Belinda.

'Just a bit,' said Holly. 'You could have been a bit more subtle about it. You virtually called her a fraud to her face.'

'Well,' said Belinda. 'She is, isn't she? Headache indeed. If she's supposed to be such a whale at curing people, how come she's suffering with a headache? Do you think I should have offered to nip down to the chemist for her and get some aspirin? Anyway, she hasn't got a headache at all, if you ask me. She just didn't want to answer any more questions.'

'It's a pity,' said Holly. 'I was thinking of buying a couple of those little tricks for Jamie.'

'Then I'm glad I got us thrown out,' said Belinda. 'Your brother is enough of a menace without you supplying him with extra ammunition. I don't want wobbly spider-things stuck down the back of my neck, thank you.'

As they were deciding what to do next a woman came out of the next shop along.

'Oh, dear,' she said, noticing the CLOSED sign in The Green Way's window. 'I've missed her.'

'She's only just closed up,' said Holly. 'You should still be able to catch her.'

'It's nothing vital,' said the woman. 'I run the shop next door. The postman delivered these to me by mistake. I've been so rushed today that I've only just had a moment to go through the post.' She held a small bundle of envelopes out. 'See?' She said. 'It's quite clear. Forty-five Radnor Street. My shop's number forty-three. I don't know what these postmen are thinking about sometimes.' She held the envelopes out to Holly. 'Be a dear and pop them through the letter-box for me, will you?'

'Of course,' said Holly. She took the letters and stooped to push them through the low letter-box at the foot of the door. As they went through she glanced at the address of the top one.

It had been redirected from London.

The letter was addressed to a Mr J Sharpe at an

address in Kennington. The London address has been crossed through and the address in Willow Dale added.

Holly stood up, frowning. The woman had gone.

'That's funny,' said Holly.

'What is?' asked Belinda.

'Well, that top letter – it was addressed to Kennington originally.'

'So?' said Belinda. 'Isn't that where Mark said they came from?'

'No. Not at all. He said they had a house in Kensington. Not Kennington.'

'Perhaps you misheard him. They sound pretty similar.'

Holly shook her head. 'No. He definitely said Kensington. Kennington is south of the river, for a start. It's a much more ordinary sort of place than Kensington.' Holly frowned. 'And the letter was for someone called Sharpe.'

'There you are then,' said Belinda. 'It wasn't for them at all. You've got the most suspicious mind sometimes, Holly.'

Holly frowned. 'I'm not so sure,' she said. 'Kennington? Kensington? And don't forget he made that mistake about Harrods being in Kensington, which means he doesn't really know the area that well.' She looked at Belinda with the gleam of a new mystery in her eyes.

'There's something very curious about all this,' she said. 'And I'm going to find out what it is.'

Belinda's forehead wrinkled. 'Oh, dear,' she sighed. 'Here we go again.'

5 The mysterious stranger

'Well,' said Miss Horswell. 'It certainly looks as if everything is coming along smoothly.' The head-teacher smiled at Miss Baker. 'Keep me informed about your progress, and let me know if you hit any snags.' She nodded towards the festival committee. 'I'm sure it'll be a great success,' she said. 'Keep up the good work.'

'There you are,' said Miss Baker after Miss Horswell had left the room. 'The seal of approval. Now then, we've still got to decide who's doing the video recording.'

It was a festival committee progress meeting in which the last few outstanding jobs were being allocated. The question of who was to record the event with the school's camcorder had come up again.

'Steffie did a good job of it last year,' said Miss Baker. 'But I'd really like someone else to be given a chance this time. What about you, Kurt? You're handy with a camera, by all accounts.'

'I won't have the time,' said Kurt. 'My dad's

asked me to take photos for the *Express*. I thought perhaps Holly might like to give it a try.'

Miss Baker looked at Holly. 'Might you?' she asked.

'I wouldn't mind,' said Holly. 'But I'm already doing the write-up for the magazine.'

'Excuse me,' said Steffie. 'I only told Holly she could do the piece for the magazine because I thought I'd be doing the videoing again. But as I'm not, I can write it myself.' She gave Holly one of her acid smiles. 'If that suits Holly, that is. Unless she wants to do *everything*.'

Holly ignored the sarcastic tone in Steffie's voice. 'I'm perfectly happy to handle the videoing,' she said. 'If someone will show me how it works.'

'That's settled, then,' said Miss Baker. 'Holly can do the recording. Perhaps you'd like to have a practice run with Steffie before the day? She'll tell you how to use it.'

Steffie gave Holly a sour look.

'That'll be fun,' Holly whispered to Belinda.

Various committee members gave updates on their progress. The painting of the canvas skirting was going well, and the woodwork department had almost finished the trees. The costumes were taking a bit longer, especially Tracy's, which was going to be very elaborate, but they were assured everything would be completed by the day of the festival.

Holly still hadn't thought of a way of mentioning to Tracy about the puzzle of Mark's London address. 'After all,' as she had said to Belinda, 'it's hardly a *crime*, is it? Even if we're right about him, all he's doing is pretending he comes from somewhere he doesn't.'

'No, it's not a crime,' Belinda had agreed. 'But it is a *lie*, and I don't like the idea of Tracy getting mixed up with someone who's quite that good at telling lies. Even if they're only white lies.'

The meeting broke up and Holly, Belinda and Tracy headed for the canteen.

'Steffie seemed very pleased with herself,' said Tracy. 'Elbowing you out of the magazine write-up.'

'Oh, I don't mind,' said Holly. 'I can't do everything, and the videoing should be fun.'

'I hope I get plenty of close-ups,' said Tracy. 'As I'm going to be the star.'

'As long as you keep it well away from me,' said Belinda.

They pushed through the canteen doors. 'Oh, look,' said Tracy. 'There's Mark. We can go and sit with him.'

They carried their trays to the table where Mark was sitting.

'Good meeting?' he asked. 'Did you get everything sorted out?'

'Yes,' said Tracy. 'Holly's doing the videoing, once she's been shown how to use the camcorder.'

'It's pretty straightforward,' said Mark. 'I can show you, if you like.'

'You know how to do *that* as well, do you?' said Belinda. 'Your talents never cease to amaze me. In fact, your whole family is amazing.'

Holly recognised the tone in Belinda's voice and gave her a kick under the table. Belinda took no notice. 'Tell me,' she said. 'Has your father ever performed on stage? In a proper theatre, I mean?'

'Plenty of times,' said Mark. 'I'm not surprised you haven't heard of him up here, but he's well-known in London.'

'Is he?' said Holly. 'That's funny. I don't think *I* ever heard of him down there.'

Mark gave her a sharp look. 'He used a different name,' he said. He took a coin out of his pocket. 'Watch this,' he said.

He passed the coin from one hand to the other, then lifted his hand to his mouth and showed the coin for a second between his teeth. He made a swallowing motion and showed them his two empty hands. Then he reached across and pulled the coin out of Belinda's ear.

Tracy laughed and clapped.

Belinda smiled. 'You're full of tricks, aren't you?' she said. 'Tricky as a fox.'

Mark grinned, but there was an unpleasant glint in his eyes.

'And he's going to teach me some tricks for the festival,' said Tracy.

'Are people really going to spot tricks like that?' asked Holly. 'I mean, you're going to be trundling by on the back of a float.'

'She's got a point,' said Mark. 'Perhaps magic tricks aren't the best idea, after all.'

'I want to do *something*,' said Tracy. 'I don't want just to be standing there smiling and waving like everyone else.'

'Juggling,' said Mark. 'People would see that all right.' He looked at Tracy. 'Do you fancy trying your hand at a spot of juggling? My mum's great at it. I'm not so hot myself, but I know how it's done.'

'I could try,' said Tracy.

'It would mean a lot of practising,' said Mark. He shook his head. 'You probably wouldn't be able to get the hang of it in time.'

Tracy's eyes glowed with the challenge. 'Wanta bet?' she said. 'You show me how it's done and I'll do it. There's nothing I can't do if I put my mind to it.'

'It's a deal,' said Mark. He stood up. 'I've got things to do,' he said. 'I'll catch you later.'

Tracy looked after him. 'He's great, isn't he?' she said. 'Real fun to be with, you know?'

'More fun than Kurt?' said Belinda.

Tracy frowned at her. 'No, not *more* fun. Different fun. I like getting to know different people. What's wrong with that?'

'Nothing,' said Belinda. 'But you don't really know him, do you? All you know is what he's chosen to tell you.'

'Belinda,' Holly warned.

'What are you trying to say?' asked Tracy. 'Is this about Kurt again? Look, I've told you, there was never anything serious between me and Kurt. Just like there's nothing serious between me and Mark. We're just friends, OK?'

'I wasn't thinking about Kurt this time,' said Belinda. 'I don't think you should believe everything Mark tells you, that's all. Like that business about his father being famous down in London. If he was so famous how come Holly had never heard of him?'

'He told you,' said Tracy, a glint of anger in her eyes. 'His father used a different name.'

'I notice he didn't tell us what this *other* name actually was,' said Belinda. 'He just did that coin trick to change the subject.'

'I'm not listening to any more of this,' said Tracy. She pushed her plate forwards and got up. 'I think you're being completely unfair to Mark. I don't know why you don't like him, but I'm not stopping here to listen to you running him down any more.'

'Don't row, you two,' said Holly. 'How about you both coming round to my place this evening? We could have another look at that file we started on the burglaries. How about it? A Mystery Club meeting.'

'Sorry,' said Tracy. 'I'm going to be busy.'

They watched as she made her way out of the canteen.

'You could have backed me up,' said Belinda. 'Why didn't you say anything about that letter?'

'Because it doesn't prove anything,' said Holly. 'Perhaps he just makes things up because he can't help himself. What's the point in you and Tracy rowing about it?'

'We wouldn't row if she wasn't so pigheaded,' said Belinda. 'Can't she see what a creep he is?'

'Even if he is, that's no reason for falling out with Tracy,' said Holly. 'I thought the three of us were going to be friends no matter what.'

'It's not my fault,' said Belinda.

'Yes, it is,' said Holly. 'It's both your faults.' Holly stood up.

'Where are you off to?' asked Belinda.

'Nowhere,' said Holly. 'Just for a walk.'

'Look,' said Belinda. 'You don't like the way he behaves any more than I do.'

'I know,' said Holly. 'But I'm not sure if it's worth all this trouble between us. I'll see you later.'

Holly made her way down to the playground.

Her suspicions about Mark were just as strong as Belinda's, but her friend's blunt way of approaching things didn't seem at all helpful. Instead of gently warning Tracy about him, all that was happening was that they were pushing Tracy away. And that was the last thing Holly wanted.

She found Jamie idly kicking a football about with a few friends. He seemed to be in a bad mood as well.

'What's wrong with everyone these days?' said Holly. 'Is it the weather, or what?'

'It's that rotten festival,' said Jamie. 'I gave them all these brilliant ideas about making monsters and alien beings for the stall, but all they want is cute little bean-bag frogs and pixies and rubbish like that. And I've got to make some plaster of Paris gnomes.'

The football came skidding towards him and he gave it a ferocious kick and pelted after it. 'I hate gnomes!' he shouted back at her.

It didn't seem to Holly that things were going to get better between her friends unless something was done to clear up this business about Mark Greenaway once and for all.

Either she needed proof that Mark was constantly lying, or some evidence to convince Belinda – and herself – that they were mistaken about him.

After all, she said to herself. *Apart from all his boasting, what has he really done? Maybe his father was well-known in London under another name? It's not impossible.*

She had an idea. It was no good asking Mark about it. But perhaps Mark's mother might say something, if she was approached in the right way.

Maybe if she went back to The Green Way, she could get into a casual conversation with Mary Greenaway. There would be nothing suspicious in asking about the Great Mysterioso. And that way, she might be able to find out if he really did use a different name in London. She might even be able to sort out the peculiar business about where they had actually lived.

Going back to the Greenaways' shop with Belinda wouldn't be a good idea. Belinda tended to be too blunt. But she could go there on her own, Holly decided. She even had an excuse. Jamie was fed up at the moment, and a few of those silly tricks would cheer him up no doubt. And while she was buying them, she could do a bit of investigating via Mary Greenaway.

After school that afternoon, Holly caught a bus to the old centre of town and made her way to Radnor Street.

She was just turning the corner when someone caught her eye. Walking briskly along the far side of the road was the man from the faith healing meeting. The man apparently crippled by arthritis who had caused such a sensation with his recovery at the very end of the meeting.

It was him, without a doubt. Marching along the pavement as if he'd never had a day's illness in his life.

Well, thought Holly. *He* would, *wouldn't he? If Mary Greenaway had cured him?'*

If she had.

If he had actually been ill in the first place.

Holly paused on the corner and watched him. He was a thin, middle-aged man with grizzled hair and a narrow, pointed face with a prominent nose and heavy jowls. He looked like a half-starved bloodhound down on his luck.

Holly's eyes widened. The man had stopped outside the Greenaways' shop and was peering in through the window. As Holly watched, Mr Greenaway, the Great Mysterioso himself, came out of the shop and the two men started talking.

After a few moments Mr Greenaway closed and locked the shop door, and the two men walked away down the street together.

Holly watched them go, her suspicions aroused. How was it that the two men knew each other? Mr Greenaway had not been at the faith healing meeting. They couldn't have met there. So how did they know each other?

It was a set-up! thought Holly. The man never

was ill. They had him planted in the audience as a final clincher for all those people who hadn't been convinced by the other 'cures' Mary Greenaway seemed to have performed.

Holly forgot her plans for talking to Mary Greenaway. She caught a bus home and telephoned Belinda.

'Can you come over?' she said. 'I've got some new information about the Greenaways. I don't want to tell you over the phone. We need to have a proper talk about it.'

Belinda said she would be there in half an hour.

Holly put the phone down and went through into the kitchen. Jamie looked up at her, his face and hands smeared with white. He was at the table, stirring a mixture with his mother's best wooden spoon in a china bowl. A bag of dry powder spilled its contents over the table.

'What a mess,' said Holly. 'What on earth are you doing?'

'Making gnomes,' said Jamie.

'Did Mum say you could use her best kitchenware for it?' asked Holly. There was white powder all down the front of Jamie's clothes and more of the stuff on the floor.

'She won't mind. I've got to do it somehow, haven't I?' said Jamie. 'What else could I use?'

Holly shook her head. 'She'll kill you. Look at the state of you!'

Jamie looked down at himself. 'It'll brush off,' he said, stirring vigorously at the thick paste.

Holly walked over to the table. 'What exactly are you up to?' she asked.

Jamie held up a saggy plastic gnome-shape. 'These are the moulds,' he said. 'I've got to pour the wet plaster into these moulds. And then, when it's gone hard, I peel the mould off and I've got a gnome, see?'

Holly frowned. 'Have you actually managed one yet?'

Jamie shook his head. He pointed to a shapeless blob that was stuck to the table. 'That was my first try,' he said. 'But I didn't give it time to dry properly so it sort of squished. That's why I'm making the stuff thicker,' he explained. 'So it'll dry quicker. I know what I'm doing.'

Holly gave him a look. 'If you're sure,' she said. She looked at the wall clock. 'Mum will be home in an hour,' she said. 'You'd better have it cleared up by then or she'll have a fit.'

'No problem,' said Jamie. 'I've got it all under control.'

Holly left him to it. She didn't want to be in the vicinity when her mother got home and found the state of the kitchen.

She went up to her room and had a look at the Mystery Club's notebook. Quite a few pages had been filled in since they had started making notes

69

of their adventures. The most recent entries were clippings from the local paper about the spate of burglaries.

Holly turned a fresh page and wrote 'Mary Greenaway, Faith Healer' at the top.

Belinda arrived a few minutes later, and Holly told her what she had seen.

'I knew it!' said Belinda. 'I knew she was a fraud all along. And this proves it. That man must be working with them. What a family! But you're not the only one who's found something out. Mary Greenaway has been going round to people's houses and giving them private treatment sessions. My mother found out from old Mrs Kellett. My mother's been visiting her recently, ever since her place was burgled, just to check she's all right. Apparently a few weeks ago she had Mary Greenaway round for a private faith healing session. And the Greenaway woman charged her for the visit and sold her masses of her herbal remedies as well. My mother told me it cost her a fortune.' Belinda looked at Holly. 'And if that isn't wrong, I'd like to know what is, especially as we now know that the whole thing is a set-up!'

'My mum *said* she'd start doing that,' said Holly. 'But I hadn't realised she was already doing it.' She frowned thoughtfully at Belinda. 'I wonder how many other people Mary Greenaway has been taking money from?'

6 A meeting with Mr Sharpe

'Jamie!' Mrs Adams's voice came up the stairs like a rifle shot. 'Get down here this instant!'

'Uh-oh!' said Holly. 'She's seen the kitchen.'

Belinda gave her a puzzled look. Holly explained about the plaster of Paris gnomes.

The two girls were stretched on the floor in Holly's bedroom with the red Mystery Club notebook open in front of them.

They had spent a long time discussing what they should do about Mary Greenaway. Belinda was all for painting a placard with the words 'MARY GREENAWAY IS A FRAUD!' and marching up and down outside the shop with it. Holly, whose father had been a solicitor in London, had pointed out that this was called libel, and that it would get them in deep trouble.

It really seemed to Holly that there was nothing they *could* do. Reluctantly she had turned the Mystery Club notebook back to their burglaries page.

The Mystery Club always kept notes about anything unusual that went on in the town. The big difference this time was that Tracy wasn't there to discuss it with them.

'If we want to investigate these break-ins properly,' said Belinda, 'we ought to go to the houses of the people burgled and ask questions. I could start off by visiting Mrs Kellett with my mother one evening.'

'I don't think people are going to be interested in being interviewed by *us*,' said Holly. 'They've probably already had enough of that with the police.'

'True,' said Belinda. 'But my mother knows everybody around where we live.' She grinned. 'My mother's the best detective of the lot of us when it comes to finding out what's going on around the town.'

'OK, then,' said Holly. 'You pump your mum for information and I'll keep the news clippings. We'll see where that gets us.' She turned the page to their new notes about the faith healing meeting.

'Poor old Mrs Kellett,' she said. 'She doesn't seem to have much luck, does she? First of all she gets ripped off by Mary Greenaway, and then she's burgled.'

'I can't believe that Mary Greenaway has only just started doing this,' said Belinda. 'It wouldn't surprise me if they've been travelling round the country ripping people off for years.' She sat up with a jerk, excitement showing on her face. 'Now *that* would explain all the nonsense from Mark about where they lived. Perhaps they're not from London at all.' Belinda's eyes gleamed. 'Maybe they go around the country, preying on sick people, taking their money and then vanishing off somewhere else before they're found out.'

'There was a London address on that letter I saw,' Holly reminded her.

Belinda slumped. 'Yes, that's true.' She sighed. 'You know what we really need here, don't you?'

'What?'

'Tracy,' said Belinda. 'It's just not the same without her. It's always Tracy who comes up with some idea out of nowhere, when we can't think of what to do.'

'We ought at least to tell Tracy what we've found out,' said Holly. 'Mark must know what's going on. We've got to warn her, whether she likes it or not.'

'I vote we tell her tomorrow,' said Belinda. 'We've got to convince her that Mark and his mother are bad news.'

The following day was a Saturday. All those involved in the school's festival preparations had been asked to attend a sort of dress rehearsal. Tracy would be there. The only question was whether they would be able to prise Tracy away from Mark for long enough to warn her about him.

They heard feet on the stairs. Holly's bedroom door opened. Mrs Adams stood there.

'Jamie tells me you knew all about what he was up to down in the kitchen, making gnomes with my best kitchenware,' she said. 'Is that true?' She was clearly angry.

'I told him he'd get into trouble,' said Holly.

'For heaven's sake,' said her mother. 'You should have stopped him. Or at least you could have helped him out. You must have seen the state he was getting in. I think you'd better come down and help clear up.'

The two girls went downstairs. Jamie was at the sink, trying vainly to hack dried lumps of plaster of Paris out of his mother's best cooking bowl.

Belinda bit her lips to stop herself laughing.

'I didn't know it was going to dry so quickly,' said Jamie.

Holly gave Belinda a despairing look. 'You don't have to stay if you don't want to,' she said. 'It looks like this is going to take hours.'

Three or four sad-looking, malformed gnomes sat dejectedly on the kitchen table. Clearly, Jamie's solo attempts at creating saleable goods for the charity stall had not proved to be a success.

'Oh, I don't mind,' said Belinda, rolling up her sleeves. 'What better way to spend a Friday evening?'

*　　*　　*

74

'Left hand down a bit,' shouted Mr Thwaites. 'A bit more. That's fine. Now, bang a nail in quick to hold it.'

Holly hammered and stepped back. The canvas sheeting sagged. Mr Thwaites jumped down from the deck of the float.

'That's the idea,' he said. 'Bang a nail in every metre or so all the way round and it'll look fine.'

It was Saturday morning at Winifred Bowen-Davies School. A frantic, hectic Saturday morning of trying to get everything looking right for the festival while at the same time coming to terms with the fact that half the things they needed weren't ready.

Holly's father and some students were busy fixing struts on to the float. These would form the foundation for the hardboard trees that were currently lying all over the playground with the paint drying on them.

Holly and Belinda and a few others were helping put the brightly painted canvas skirt round the base of the float, while Mr Thwaites and Mr Barnard, the art teacher, shouted instructions.

A small group from the music club were playing a bouncy dance tune and a troupe of first formers were practising morris-dancing. Belinda had nearly laughed herself into a seizure watching them before she had been whisked off to help with some of the costumes that the older students would be wearing.

The question of who was to play the jester had finally been resolved. Miss Baker had tried the three-cornered cap with its jingling bells on several heads before she had found a perfect fit.

'You're kidding!' said Belinda, shaking her head so that the bells chimed around her ears. 'How did I get lumbered with this?'

'Just your good luck,' Miss Baker said with a laugh. She handed Belinda a stick with a balloon tied to the end. 'Now practise going around hitting people with the balloon.' She patted Belinda's cheeks with both hands. 'It suits you,' she said. 'You could have been born for it.'

Belinda gave Miss Baker a swipe with the balloon.

Helpful hands stretched the canvas as Holly went round the float with her hammer and nails. She felt something hit her behind. She looked round to find Belinda standing there in a red and white smock and the jester's hat. Belinda batted her over the head with her balloon.

'I could get used to this,' she said. 'How do I look?'

'It's an improvement,' said Holly. She looked around the busy playground. 'Have you seen anything of Tracy?'

'She's inside somewhere, having her costume fitted,' said Belinda.

'And Mark?' asked Holly.

Belinda shook her head. 'I haven't seen him all morning.'

'Hang on a minute while I finish this,' said Holly. 'And then we can go and find Tracy, OK?'

While Holly banged in the final few nails, Belinda amused herself by ballooning anyone who came within reach.

The two friends made their way up the main steps into the school. Belinda stood under the sombre portrait of the school's founder – Winifred Bowen-Davies herself.

'Who are you looking at?' said Belinda, giving the solemn face a tap with her balloon. 'I may look like an idiot now, but don't forget it was us who found that hidden painting behind you.'

Holly smiled. 'And helped pay for the new gym out of the proceeds,' she said. 'Our first mystery. Remember how Tracy – '

'Ahem!'

They spun round. Mr Kerwood, the deputy headteacher stood in the hallway.

'Miss Baker's orders,' Belinda said with a grin. 'I'm to hit everyone I see.'

Mr Kerwood wandered off without comment.

Belinda pulled a face. 'Clearly not amused,' she said.

'Let's find Tracy,' said Holly. 'I want to get this over with.'

One classroom had been given over to the group who were dealing with the costumes. The plan was for the musicians to sit on the back end of the float and play while the morris-dancing team followed on behind. After that would come several other characters, including the jester.

Some of the costumes were of animals and some were meant to be people from the Middle Ages.

Holly and Belinda looked in through the door. A cleverly-designed stag's head mask looked round at them, the antlers made from wire wrapped with papier-mâché.

Tracy was standing on a desk in her costume while a couple of girls were tacking up the hem.

The costume was very impressive. Originally a floor-length white shift, it had been covered all over with trailing strips of highly-coloured material. Tracy looked like a cross between a midsummer flower-bed and an exotic bird, completely enclosed in the costume so that only her head showed.

'Wow!' said Belinda.

Tracy smiled and lifted her arms, the full sleeves spreading out like rainbow-coloured wings.

'Pretty neat, huh?' she said. 'Am I gorgeous or what?'

The two girls came into the room.

'Is the head-dress finished yet?' asked Holly.

'It sure is,' said Tracy, pointing to another desk. On it lay the crowning glory of the festival queen's costume – a mask in the shape of a sun with golden rays fanning out of it.

Tracy jumped down from the desk and carefully fitted the mask over her head. Her face was completely hidden except for two slots through which her blue eyes sparkled.

'Excellent,' said Mrs Bannister, who had guided the making of the outfit. 'Give us a twirl.'

Tracy spun in a fluttering swarm of colour, the golden mask gleaming in the light.

'OK,' said Mrs Bannister. 'Take it off now, Tracy, and we'll tack up that hem. And then it'll be finished.'

Holly and Belinda helped Tracy out of her costume.

'Phew!' she puffed. 'It's going to be pretty warm in there if it's a sunny day. How are things going outside?'

'Chaotic,' said Holly. 'Come and see.'

The three girls stood on the school steps and watched as the hardboard trees were lifted one by one up on to the float and screwed into position by Holly's father.

'We wanted a word with you, actually,' said Holly. 'About Mark.'

Tracy smiled. 'Let's not argue about him, huh?' she said. 'It's too nice a day for a row.'

'There are things you don't know about him,' said Belinda.

Tracy sighed. 'OK,' she said. 'Spit it out. He's on the run from the police – is that it? Or . . . let me think . . . he's involved with a white-slave gang and he's planning on kidnapping us and selling us abroad. Am I getting warm?'

Holly told her about the 'healed' man that she had seen with Mark's father, and about Mary Greenaway charging money for private healing sessions.

Tracy became quiet. 'But all the same,' she said thoughtfully. 'Even if you're right – that's not *Mark*. That's just his mom behaving badly. If it's true. You can't blame Mark for that.'

'But he must know about it,' said Belinda.

'Maybe he does,' said Tracy. 'But what would you expect him to do? He can't help it if his mom is working some scam.'

'But he's also lied about where they come from,' said Belinda. Holly gave Belinda an expressive look, wishing she had broken that bit of news a little less bluntly.

'What do you mean?' asked Tracy. 'Why do you say that?'

'I saw a letter,' said Holly. 'Redirected from London. It was from Kennington – not Kensington. It's a completely different place.'

'If he's lying about where they come from,' said

80

Belinda, 'what else is he lying about? You can't trust him, Tracy. You really ought to keep away from him.'

Tracy frowned at them. 'You haven't liked him from the moment you set eyes on him,' she said. 'I don't know why, but you've been against him from the start.' She looked at Holly. 'How would you have liked it if everyone had been spreading rumours about you when you first came here? I think you're both being totally unfair.' She ran back into the school. 'I don't want to hear another word from either of you about him,' she called back. 'I thought you were my *friends*.'

Holly and Belinda looked at each other.

Holly frowned. 'I think we've made it worse,' she said.

Belinda tapped her balloon dismally on the ground. 'Now what do we do?' she said.

'If we could just nail down *one* of Mark's lies we might be able to get Tracy on our side,' said Holly. 'I still think we should try and get some information out of Mary Greenaway about that other name Mark said his father was known by in London. I'm absolutely convinced he wasn't telling the truth about that.'

'Rather you than me,' said Belinda.

Holly turned to look at her, a familiar gleam in her eyes. 'We're both doing it,' she said. 'We'll go to the shop this afternoon.'

81

Belinda lifted her balloon and bounced it bleakly on Holly's head. 'The things you get me into,' she said with a sigh.

'Do you want a lift home?' asked Mr Adams. All the work that could be done on the float had been finished and the workers were leaving. The float was parked up against the school wall with a protective plastic canopy over it.

The costumes had been put away. Holly and Belinda hadn't seen Tracy again after their uncomfortable conversation with her.

'No thanks,' said Holly. 'We thought we'd do a bit of window-shopping in town.'

'Fair enough,' said her father, climbing into his Range Rover. 'See you later, then.' He grinned at Belinda. 'By the way, I thought the jester's costume suited you a treat.'

'Everyone's said that,' complained Belinda. 'Do you think people are trying to tell me something?'

The two girls caught a bus into town.

The sunny Saturday afternoon had brought people out in droves. The whole area around the old church was crowded with people meandering happily along, enjoying the sights and sounds of the picturesque old heart of Willow Dale.

The Greenaways' shop seemed to be doing a good trade. There was only one problem. It wasn't Mary Greenaway behind the counter. It was Mark.

'Now what do we do?' whispered Belinda, as she and Holly stood by the rack of tricks.

'Buy some tricks for Jamie,' said Holly. 'That was going to be my excuse anyway.'

She chose a couple of packets she thought her brother would like.

'Right,' said Holly. 'I know something I *can* ask him. Let's see how he gets out of this.'

They went up to the counter.

'Hello,' said Mark. 'Sorry I couldn't make it to the school to help out. We've been a bit busy here. How did it go?'

'Fine,' said Holly. She glanced round. There was no one close by. 'I want to talk to you.'

Mark smiled. 'Talk away.'

'We were at your mother's meeting the other night,' said Holly. 'She healed a man of arthritis. Or so she said.' She looked round again to make sure she was not being overheard. 'I saw the same man here with your father yesterday.' She paused.

'Yes?' said Mark. 'I'm with you so far. So what's the problem?'

'The problem is,' said Holly, 'if he was supposed to be some complete stranger, how come he was round here chatting to your father a couple of days later?'

A huge grin spread over Mark's face. 'I get it,' he said. 'You think it was a put-up job?'

'Well?' said Belinda. 'Was it?'

'Not at all,' Mark said smoothly. 'The guy was down on his luck. It's not easy to get work when you're doubled up with arthritis. He stayed on at the hall to thank my mother after everyone else had gone, and she found out he had nowhere to go and no money.' Mark smiled. 'So she offered him a job here. Stay put and I'll introduce you. He's just round the back.'

Mark went through to the back of the shop. Holly and Belinda looked at each other uncomfortably.

A few seconds later Mark reappeared, and behind him was the thin-faced man from the faith healing meeting.

'Joe, I'd like you to meet Holly and Belinda,' said Mark. 'They're friends of mine from school.'

'Pleased to meet you,' said the man. 'The name's Joe Sharpe.'

'I hope you're still feeling well,' said Belinda.

'This is the first time I've been out of pain for ten years,' said Joe Sharpe. 'Thanks to Mrs Greenaway I've got my health and a place of work.' He looked at Mark. 'I can't thank your mother enough. She's a miracle worker.'

Mark gave the girls a questioning look.

'I'm very happy for you,' said Holly. She looked at Mark. 'I'll just pay for these, then,' she said.

Belinda and Holly stood outside the shop.

'You didn't believe that, did you?' said Belinda.

Holly shook her head. 'I might have done if

84

I hadn't seen the name on that envelope the other day.'

'What name?'

Holly stared back into the shop. 'Don't you remember?' she asked. 'That letter from Kennington was addressed to a Mr J. Sharpe. Joe Sharpe. Even if I was crazy enough to believe a story like that, it all falls to pieces if our Mr Sharpe was already receiving redirected mail here the day after the meeting.'

She looked at Belinda. 'Now we *know* it's a con. The question is – what do we do about it?'

7 Burglaries close to home

'Belinda! Belinda! Wake up, we've been burgled!'

Belinda rolled over in bed, mumbling to herself and trying to shake off the hand that was clamped on her shoulder.

The dream had taken a curious turn.

It was the grand finale at the Olympic horse trials. Meltdown had sailed over the jumps as if he had wings. He had made a perfect turn into the run up to the wall.

And then Belinda's mother was on Meltdown with her, tugging at her shoulder.

'Mum! Get off!'

'Belinda! Wake up! We've been burgled.'

Belinda sat up in a tangle of bedclothes. She blinked at her mother and automatically reached for her glasses. 'What?'

Her mother was in her dressing-gown, her usually immaculate hair ruffled and sticking up in porcupine quills.

'I've just been downstairs,' said Mrs Hayes. 'We've had burglars overnight.'

'You're kidding!' said Belinda.

Her mother gave her an expressive look. 'I'm going to phone the police,' she said. 'Get yourself dressed.'

Belinda slung on her old jeans and baggy green sweatshirt.

Her mother sat on her bed. 'Where in the name of sanity is your telephone?' The two of them stared down at the chaos that swarmed over Belinda's floor. 'What is the point of you having an extension up here if a person can never find the telephone when it's needed?'

'Calm down,' said Belinda soothingly. She found the wire and traced it to the receiver. 'I know where everything is.' She put the telephone in her mother's lap.

'Is there much damage downstairs?' she asked.

'Go and see for yourself.'

Belinda padded downstairs cautiously, as if she expected burglars to leap out at her at any moment.

The front door was slightly ajar. Coats and bags were strewn on the floor. Drawers had been taken out of cabinets and left on the carpet with their contents up-ended.

Belinda wandered dazedly around the ground floor. Every room showed signs of having been ransacked.

She went through into the long back room. A cool early-morning breeze was drifting in through an open side of the French windows.

'Don't touch anything.'

Belinda looked round. Her mother was standing in the doorway. 'The police said not to touch anything.'

'I wasn't going to,' said Belinda. She looked at her mother. 'I didn't hear a sound.' She shivered. 'They were down here, going through our stuff, and I didn't hear a single solitary sound. That's so creepy.'

'They must have known there were people in the place,' said Mrs Hayes. 'There's no sign of them having gone upstairs. Thank heavens.' She sat on a chair. 'I feel quite unwell,' she said.

'Shall I get you some aspirin?'

'I told your father we should get an alarm system,' said Belinda's mother.

'Or a big, fierce dog,' said Belinda. 'They wouldn't have hung around long with a decent-sized set of teeth in the seat of their trousers. Have you had a proper look round yet, to see what's missing?'

'I haven't had time. I'm going up to get dressed, dear. Listen for the bell, will you? They're sending an officer round.' Her mother trailed upstairs.

Belinda walked around the downstairs rooms with her hands in her pockets. She felt that she wanted to *do* something. Thieves had broken in during the night and all they could do was to stand around helplessly waiting for the police.

Belinda went into the hall. 'Can I phone Holly?' she called. There was no answer from upstairs.

She shrugged and picked up the phone.

'So what did the police say?' asked Holly. She and Belinda were sitting in the Hayeses' kitchen, nibbling toast and drinking coffee. Belinda's mother was in another room, telephoning credit card companies and insurance firms.

'Not a lot,' said Belinda. 'The officer said it was probably an amateur job. He reckons they were just looking for money. They left a lot of valuable stuff untouched. He said professionals would have taken all the antiques and silver stuff, but this lot just seemed to grab whatever came to hand. They've taken my mother's bag, of course, with all her credit cards and things in it. They got in through the French windows and out through the front. They broke a glass panel in the back and just reached through and undid the bolt. As easy as that. He said they were probably in and out in fifteen minutes. They're sending round a home security officer to give us some tips on how to make sure it doesn't happen again.'

'Did he take fingerprints?' asked Holly.

'No. Apparently the fingerprint people don't work on Sundays. They're coming round first thing tomorrow. In the meantime we've got to leave everything the way it is.'

A familiar light came into Holly's eyes. 'That gives us the rest of the day to look round for clues,' she said.

'We mustn't touch anything,' said Belinda.

'That doesn't stop us looking,' said Holly. 'Do they think it's the same lot who have been doing the other break-ins around here? I suppose it must be.'

'I suppose so,' said Belinda. 'He didn't say. He just said we should make a list of everything that was missing. I'm not going to be much use there. I've never paid much attention to all the bits and pieces my parents keep buying.' She drank up her coffee. 'Do you want to have a look round, then?'

Holly rummaged in her bag and brought out the Mystery Club notebook. 'We can write down everything we find that looks suspicious,' she said.

They went through into the long back room with the French windows. The damage caused by the burglars was obvious. A small pane of glass at the top of the left-hand door was broken. Shards of glass littered the carpet. Holly knelt to look closely at them, not really sure what she was hoping to see.

'It feels funny doing this without Tracy,' said Belinda. 'I keep expecting to hear her say, "Hey, you guys, look what I've found."' Belinda did a passable imitation of Tracy's American accent.

Holly looked up. 'I know what you mean,' she said. 'And she'd be furious at being left out.'

Belinda nibbled her lip. 'Shall I phone her?'

Holly grinned. 'Yes. That's a good idea. The three of us are still the Mystery Club, after all. And it'll give us a chance to make up with her.'

Holly breathed a sigh of relief as Belinda went off to phone. After all the adventures they'd had together, it would be terrible for them to fall out permanently over someone like Mark Greenaway. Especially now that Belinda's own house had been burgled.

'No luck,' said Belinda, coming back in. She slumped in a chair. 'She's out. I spoke to her mother.' She gave Holly a look. 'And guess who she's out with?'

Holly nodded. 'Mark, I suppose.'

'Got it in one,' said Belinda. 'The deeply unconvincing Mark Greenaway.'

Holly stood up. 'Let's carry on looking round,' she said. 'We can fill Tracy in on anything we find later.'

Belinda looked morosely at her. 'That's if she's interested,' she said.

They ended up spending the morning helping Belinda's mother with her list of missing valuables, but nothing useful in the way of clues that might lead to the capture of the burglars came to light.

*   *   *

'What's the news?' asked Mr Adams when Holly got home.

'Nothing much,' said Holly. 'Belinda thinks they should get themselves a guard dog.'

Jamie's ears pricked up. 'Can we get a guard dog?' he said. 'A rottweiler, or something?'

'We are not having a dog,' said Mrs Adams. 'We've got plenty of locks and bolts around the place. I'm not having everything covered in dog hair, thank you very much.'

'I could keep it in my room,' said Jamie. 'I'd look after it.'

'No,' Mrs Adams said emphatically. 'No dogs. We'll get you a gerbil if you want something to look after.'

Jamie gave her a caustic look. 'A guard gerbil?' he said. 'That's not going to frighten anyone off.' He brightened. 'Couldn't we set a trap?'

'No,' said his mother. 'No traps either.' She looked at Holly. 'How are they taking it?'

'They don't seem too upset, considering,' said Holly. She looked anxiously at her mother. 'You don't think we'll get burgled, do you?'

'They seem to be concentrating on the big houses in Belinda's neck of the woods,' said Mrs Adams. 'I think we should be safe enough if we keep everything locked up.'

'Are you going to help me with those plaster gnomes?' Jamie asked Holly.

'Not now,' said Holly. 'I've got other things to do.' She grinned at her mother. 'You never know,' she said. 'If we did have burglars, they might take Jamie away. Now that wouldn't be so bad.'

Tracy came running up to Belinda and Holly the next morning at school.

'It's terrible,' she said. 'My mom told me all about it last night. I was going to ring, but she said I shouldn't disturb you. Did they take much?'

Belinda and Holly told her everything that had gone on the previous day.

'You're lucky they didn't go upstairs,' said Tracy with a shudder. 'Imagine lying asleep in your bed with people like that creeping through the house.'

'And to think we were looking at our burglary notes only a couple of nights before,' said Holly. 'I never dreamed we'd suddenly find ourselves in the middle of it all.'

'I hope the police come up with something pretty quickly,' said Belinda. 'Solving mysteries is one thing, but this is a bit too close to home for my liking.'

Tracy looked thoughtfully at them. 'You two guys were talking over the burglaries the other evening, were you?'

'You were invited to the meeting,' said Belinda. 'You couldn't make it, remember?'

Tracy nodded. 'That was kind of silly of me. I

93

wasn't really busy. I was just so mad at you because of the bad things you were saying about Mark.'

'What bad things were these?' They looked round at the unexpected voice. Mark had come up behind them while they were speaking.

'Oh, nothing,' said Tracy. 'Belinda's house has been burgled.'

Mark stared at them. 'What?'

Tracy nodded. 'It's true,' she said. 'Saturday night.'

'Saturday night?' said Mark. He shook his head. 'Weird.'

'Why weird?' said Belinda. 'This is about the fifth burglary in the last month or so.'

'How did they get in?' asked Mark.

'They broke a window at the back,' said Belinda.

'We think it must be the same lot that have done all the other break-ins around here,' said Holly.

'Yes,' said Mark. 'I suppose it must be. They broke a window, you said?'

'That's right,' said Belinda. 'How else would they get in? They're not going to stroll in through the front door, are they?'

Mark frowned. 'No, I suppose not,' he said. 'Did they take much?'

'They missed a lot of the really valuable things,' said Belinda. 'The policeman who came round seemed to think they didn't have much of a clue. Professionals would have bagged the lot, apparently, so we've got that to be grateful for. We're having new locks put on everywhere as soon as we can, so they won't get a second chance.'

'I shouldn't worry about that,' said Mark. 'Burglars don't come back to the same place twice, do they?'

'Oddly enough the policeman said the exact opposite,' said Belinda. 'Apparently it's quite common for burglars to come back to a place quite soon after an initial break-in, especially if they've seen plenty of valuable stuff. They come back with a nice big van to cart it all away. That's why we're having a security officer round this evening.'

Mark shook his head. 'They're just telling you that so you'll spend a fortune on locks and alarms. I don't reckon they'll be back.'

'You know all about it, do you?' said Belinda. 'Something else you're an authority on, eh?'

Mark shrugged. 'It stands to reason they wouldn't risk coming back,' he said. 'I shouldn't worry about it if I were you.'

'I'll bear that in mind,' said Belinda.

'Anyway,' said Mark. 'I've got things to do. I'll catch you later.'

'I thought you were going to help me with my juggling practice?' said Tracy.

'Oh. Yes. Can we do that later? I've just got to phone home.' He smiled. 'I'll see you at break,

OK?' He walked off, leaving the three girls together.

'I wish I'd been there yesterday to help you two look around,' said Tracy. 'You know what dummies you are at spotting things. I bet I'd have found some invaluable clue.'

'You *could* have been there,' said Belinda. 'We phoned you. It's not our fault you were out with Mark.'

'He was teaching me to juggle,' explained Tracy. 'Look, can't we just forget about Mark? I want the three of us to be friends again. All we seem to do these days is argue. Can't we get back to the way we used to be? I'm not asking you to *like* the guy, but couldn't you kind of back off a bit?'

'Mark's mother is a cheat,' said Belinda.

'Yes, so you said. And maybe Mark doesn't always tell the truth. Come on, you guys, I don't believe every word he says, but he's really not that bad if you give him a chance. Hey, let's forget about him, huh?'

'That sounds like a good idea,' said Holly. She smiled at Tracy. 'The Mystery Club doesn't seem to work very well when it's just two of us.' She looked encouragingly at Belinda. 'And we've got plenty of work ahead of us if we're going to find out find out who's doing these burglaries.'

Belinda laughed. 'OK,' she said. 'No more arguments. I shan't say another word about Mark

Greenaway. Holly's right, we've got more important things to think about.' She looked at Tracy. 'How's the juggling coming along, by the way?'

'It's more difficult than I'd thought,' said Tracy. She made juggling motions with her hands. 'I can manage two balls, but you're supposed to use three.' She sighed. 'The third one's the killer. I don't know how I'm going to get it together by Saturday.'

As they were speaking, the bell went for morning registration. The three reconciled friends joined the flood of students heading for their classrooms.

Holly woke suddenly and sharply in the middle of the night, convinced she had heard a noise. She sat up, ears straining at the silence. All she could hear were her own heartbeats, sounding like hammers in her ears.

It was all Jamie's fault. He'd gone on and on about burglars that evening. It was almost as if he really *wanted* them to be burgled. As if it would be fun.

It didn't feel to Holly like something that would be fun at all. Quite the opposite. Strange, dangerous people tiptoeing around the house in the dead of night. Going through your belongings . . .

Holly wished this was one of those nights when Tracy and Belinda were staying the night. She wouldn't feel half so nervous if she had them with her. But on her own . . . well, it was all too easy for someone with Holly's fertile imagination to people the house with intruders.

She started. Was that something? A sound from downstairs? Or was it the wind rattling a window?

She slipped out of bed and drew her dressing-gown on. She padded to the door and listened intently.

This is just silly, she said to herself. She took a deep breath. *I'm going to go downstairs and get myself a drink of water. That's all I'm going to do. There aren't any burglars. There's nothing going on down there. It's all in my imagination.*

She opened her bedroom door and walked softly across the hall to the stairs. The stairwell was a pool of eerie shadows. Still, silent, watching shadows.

She crept down the stairs.

Near the bottom of the stairs she suddenly felt something against her foot, jerking it to an unexpected stop. Unable to stop herself, she pitched headlong into the hall with a scream.

There was a tumultuous crash behind her and as she sprawled helplessly on the floor she heard the clatter of running feet.

8 Holly's theory

'What on earth is going on down there?' It was Mr Adams's voice from the top of the stairs. Holly rolled over and sat up as her father switched the light on.

'It's me,' called Holly. 'I fell . . . and . . . ' she stared. In the light, the reason for her fall and for all the noise that had come after it was revealed.

A trip-wire, loosened by Holly's impact, was stretched across the stairs, three treads up from the bottom. One end of the tripwire had been attached to a stool on which someone had piled saucepans and frying pans. As her foot had come into contact with the wire, it had jerked the stool and the pots and pans had come clattering down on to the floor.

'Is it a burglar? Have we caught a burglar?' It was Jamie's voice.

Holly rubbed a painful knee. She saw Jamie's face peering eagerly over the banisters.

'You maniac!' she said. 'Did you do this?'

'Oh, it's only you,' said Jamie.

'Holly?' Mrs Adams appeared at the head of the stairs. 'What do you think you're doing making all this noise in the middle of the night?'

'Me?' gasped Holly. 'It wasn't *me*. I came down for a glass of water.'

'Jamie?' Their father's voice had a seldom-heard dangerous rumble in it.

'It was for burglars,' said Jamie. 'I wasn't expecting Holly to be clodhopping around. It was a trap for burglars in case they came upstairs. It's not my fault she fell over it.'

'Jamie, for heaven's sake,' said Mrs Adams, coming downstairs. 'Someone could have broken their neck. Of all the stupid ideas.'

'It worked, though, didn't it?' said Jamie. 'If Holly had been a burglar we'd have caught her red-handed.'

'You absolute menace,' said Holly. 'I'll kill you.'

'No need for that,' said Mr Adams. 'Jamie. Bed. I'll deal with you in the morning.' He gave Jamie a ferocious look. 'And we'll have no more bright ideas, got me?'

'Yes, Dad,' mumbled Jamie. He looked hopefully at his father. 'But it did work.'

His father pointed a stern finger. 'Bed!' he said.

'Are you in one piece?' Mrs Adams asked Holly.

'More or less – no thanks to *him*.'

Mr Adams came down the stairs, his shoulders shaking with suppressed laughter. 'You've got to admit,' he said softly, 'there's no fear of anyone getting bored in this house.'

Mrs Adams looked at the fallen pots and pans and shook her head.

'It's not funny,' said Holly. 'It frightened the life out of me. That kid ought to be kept in a zoo.'

'I'll clear up,' said Mrs Adams. 'You get your drink and get yourself back to bed, Holly.'

On her way up Holly stuck her head round Jamie's bedroom door. 'You wait 'til I get you on my own,' she threatened into the darkness. 'I'll murder you.'

She went back to bed, rubbing her sore knee and plotting revenge.

'You wait until I find him,' Holly said to Belinda and Tracy. 'He managed to sneak out this morning before I could get my hands on him. But he's not going to be able to avoid me forever. And then . . . ' She made strangling motions with her hands.

It had been a struggle for Holly to get up that morning. She'd lain awake half the night with a painful knee after encountering her brother's burglar trap. There was limited comfort in Jamie being grounded by his parents for two days as a warning not to set up any more burglar traps, but Holly still needed to give him a good shouting at before she'd feel any better.

Jamie had avoided her before school, but now

101

that it was break, Holly was determined to hunt him down.

Belinda heaved a sigh. 'It must be fun having a younger brother to beat up,' she said.

'You can have him,' said Holly. 'If there's anything left of him by the time I'm finished.'

'He was only trying to be helpful,' Tracy said with a grin. 'It was a pretty neat idea.'

'You wouldn't say that if you'd been thrown down the stairs by it,' said Holly.

She stood scanning the playground. A group of her brother's friends were having their usual kick about, but Jamie wasn't with them.

'Hunt the Jamie,' Holly said determinedly. 'Coming?'

'I don't think so,' said Belinda. 'I faint at the sight of blood.'

Holly left her friends. It took her some minutes to track Jamie down. He was over by the tennis courts, sitting alone on a low wall, staring at his shoes.

'Right, you,' said Holly. 'I want a word with you.'

Jamie looked miserably up at her.

Her vengeful mood changed immediately. 'What's up?'

'Nothing,' mumbled Jamie.

'Oh, come on,' said Holly. 'You're not sulking because Mum grounded you for a couple of days, are you? What did you expect? You'd have got it worse if she'd been the one you caught instead of me.'

'It's nothing to do with that,' Jamie said morosely.

There was obviously something wrong. All thoughts of revenge gone, Holly sat down next to him. 'What is it, then?'

'I've had my pocket money nicked,' said Jamie. '*That's* what's wrong, if you must know.'

'Have you reported it to a teacher?' asked Holly. 'Where did you lose it?'

'I didn't *lose* it,' said Jamie. 'It was taken off me.'

'By whom?' asked Holly.

'That Mark Greenaway,' Jamie said bitterly.

Holly stared at him, dumbfounded for a moment. 'Mark Greenaway stole your money?'

Jamie gave her a sideways glance. 'More or less. He cheated me. He was showing some people a game with three cards. Two ordinary ones and a Queen. He'd put them face down then move them around and get you to guess where the Queen was. It looked easy. I got it right every time. Then he bet me my pocket money I wouldn't be able to find it. He said if I got it right he'd give me twice the money.'

'Oh, Jamie, you idiot. You played the three-card trick with him? What's Mum always told you about gambling?'

'It didn't seem like gambling,' mumbled Jamie. 'I'm sure I got it right – but he switched them somehow. He's a cheat.'

'You should tell your form teacher,' said Holly. 'Mark can't be allowed to get away with things like that.'

Jamie shook his head. 'I'm not going running to a teacher,' he said. 'What do you think I am, a sneak?'

Holly stood up. 'Well, if you're not going to do anything, I am,' she said.

It wasn't difficult finding Mark. He was sitting with a ring of other boys on the grassy slope up near the back of the school. They were playing cards.

'I want a word with you,' said Holly.

Mark looked up. 'Fire away,' he said.

'In private,' said Holly.

'I'm a bit busy right now, Holly. Can't it wait?' said Mark.

'No,' said Holly.

Mark got up and Holly led him a little way off from the group of boys.

'I want Jamie's money back,' said Holly. 'He might be daft enough to think that three-card trick of yours is fair, but you and I know better, don't we?'

'No one forced him to play,' said Mark. 'He'd have made twice as much money if he'd won.'

104

'Except that there was no way for him to win,' said Holly. 'You're too good at it.'

Mark smiled. 'So he's sent big sister to get his money back,' said Mark. He reached into his pocket and tipped a handful of coins into Holly's outstretched hand.

'He didn't send me,' said Holly. 'But I don't see why you should be allowed to get away with cheating people.'

'I can do without the lecture,' said Mark. 'You've got his money back.'

'Why do you do it?' asked Holly. 'Why do you behave like this?'

Mark shrugged and turned away.

'I know you don't come from Kensington,' said Holly. 'And I know the truth about that Joe Sharpe business.'

His back was turned as she said this, so she couldn't see his immediate reaction, and by the time he turned to face her again his expression was unreadable.

'I don't know what you're talking about,' he said.

'I saw a letter for your shop,' said Holly. 'Redirected from Kennington and addressed to a Mr J. Sharpe, so don't bother lying about it.'

'You're quite the little sleuth, aren't you?' said Mark. 'What else do you do? Apart from nosing into people's mail?'

'I wasn't *nosing*. I saw it by accident,' said Holly.

'I bet you did,' said Mark scathingly. 'Accidentally on purpose, you mean. And now you think you've got it all figured out.'

'Haven't I?' said Holly.

Mark glared at her. 'I don't have to explain *anything* to you,' he said. 'But if you want to know the truth, I'll tell you. Joe wrote to my mother in London when we were living down there. He wanted to meet her, to see if she could do anything about his arthritis. She wanted to help, but we moved up here before there was a chance to see him. So we arranged for him to come up here and stay with us. That's the truth.'

'So why the pretence about not knowing him before the meeting?' asked Holly.

'We *didn't* know him,' said Mark. 'He arrived on the evening of the meeting. We'd never seen him before.'

Holly looked thoughtfully at him. Her memory of the meeting was too clear for her to be convinced by this.

She shook her head. 'Your mother pretended she knew nothing about him,' she said.

Mark smiled coldly, staring out past her shoulder. 'I'm bored with this,' he said. 'I've told you the truth. If you don't believe me, that's your problem. I've got better things to do than stand here answering your stupid questions.'

And with that, he went back to the circle of boys on the grass and carried on with the card game as if nothing had happened.

It was lunch-time when the news began to circulate of another burglary. A boy called Matthew Cooper was telling people how his house had been broken into the previous evening.

Belinda knew the family, as she did most of the families who lived in the big houses over on the rich side of Willow Dale. The Coopers lived only a couple of streets away from Belinda, and Matthew's mother was on several of Mrs Hayes's charity committees.

Towards the end of the lunch period Holly and Belinda went to have a chat with Matthew. Belinda particularly wanted to know whether his burglary had been similar to her own.

Matthew seemed perfectly happy to talk about it. Holly jotted his comments down in the Mystery Club notebook as he spoke.

'The really peculiar thing,' he told them, 'is that there was no sign of how they got in. My dad disturbed them, you see. He heard a noise and went downstairs to investigate. But they must have heard him, because they'd made a run for it by the time he got down there. They'd escaped out through the front door.' He grinned. 'They didn't get anything at all.'

'There wasn't a broken window or anything?' asked Belinda.

'No. Nothing. The police reckon my gran must have accidentally left the front door open earlier that evening when she let that faith healing woman out. My gran's getting a bit forgetful like that. The other day she – '

'The faith healing woman?' interrupted Holly. 'You mean Mary Greenaway?'

'Is that her name? I don't know. Gran had her round yesterday evening for some sort of consultation or something. My dad thinks it's all rubbish, but apparently Gran heard that she could make people better. Gran's got rheumatism. Anyway, like I was saying, the police reckon Gran forgot to shut the door properly and the burglars just strolled in.'

The bell went for afternoon lessons. There was no time to talk things over right then, but they decided to hold a Mystery Club meeting at Belinda's house after school and have a proper discussion.

They told Tracy about the meeting.

'I'm sorry,' she said. 'I really can't make it. I'm not being awkward. I've got to practise this juggling or I'm never going to get it right in time. Tell me all about it tomorrow. And I promise, once the festival is over, I'll be right there with you.'

The two girls headed for Belinda's house.

Belinda insisted on going and seeing Meltdown, who had his own stables at the far end of the Hayeses' enormous garden.

'I'm not sure it makes sense, you know,' said Holly as they brushed Meltdown's high chestnut flanks. 'This business about the grandmother leaving the door open. It's too much of a coincidence that the burglars should just happen to be passing by on that particular night.'

'You heard what Matthew said,' said Belinda, dragging the tangles out of Meltdown's long mane. 'There was no other way that they could have got in. It had to be via the front door.'

'Maybe they had a key,' said Holly.

'Don't be daft,' said Belinda. 'How would they get a key?'

'I don't know,' said Holly. 'I'm just exploring all the angles. I was thinking about it this afternoon. Matthew said the burglars were disturbed, right? Well, think about this. The burglars somehow get their hands on the key to the house. They get in through the front door, but before they make off with the stuff, they break a window or something. That way no one can guess how they really got in. Do you see what I mean?'

Belinda's round face appeared under Meltdown's neck. 'So, oh great detective,' she said, 'how do they get their hands on a key in the first place?' Her eyes suddenly narrowed. 'Mark's father had my keys that evening when he did his Great Mysterioso bit at the party.'

'And Mary Greenaway was at the Coopers' house the evening that they were burgled. And she visited that Mrs Kellett you told me about. Was she burgled before or after Mary Greenaway's visit?'

'After, I think,' said Belinda.

'That makes at least three burglaries at houses where the Greenaways had been,' said Holly. 'We've been looking at this all wrong. It's not Mary Greenaway's faith healing that's the real crime. It's the burglaries. They're involved with the burglaries.'

'Hold on a minute,' said Belinda, shaking her head. 'Mr Greenaway had my keys for only a minute or two. There's no way he could have copied them. It's a nice theory, Holly, but it doesn't really work. Besides, there have been half a dozen burglaries in the area recently.'

'Yes,' Holly said thoughtfully. 'And they started just after the Greenaways arrived in Willow Dale. And how do we know Mary Greenaway hasn't visited the other houses as well? It would be a brilliant plan. Mary Greenaway goes to a house for a session of faith healing, steals a key, and they come back later and turn the place over.'

'Matthew didn't mention that any keys were missing,' said Belinda. 'And my key wasn't stolen,

110

was it? You're letting your imagination run riot again, Holly.' Belinda's mouth fell open. 'Oh!' she gasped.

'What?'

'I've just remembered something,' said Belinda. 'Our front door has got one of those double locks on it. You know, the sort where you turn the key in the latch on the inside so no one can break a pane of glass in the door and reach through to open it. And my mother always double locks it before she goes to bed. So how was it that the burglars managed to get out through the front door? I'm sure my mother takes the keys up to her bedroom with her at night. But they must have used a key to get out!'

Holly's eyes brightened. 'So my theory could still be right.'

'I think we should go and tell my mother about this,' said Belinda.

They ran helter-skelter up the long lawn to the house.

'Mum!' shouted Belinda. They ran through the kitchen and into the hall.

Belinda's mother was standing in the hallway, speaking on the telephone. She waved at them to be quiet and the two breathless girls stood panting, waiting impatiently to get her attention.

Belinda's mother was smiling. 'Thank you,' she said into the telephone. 'That's marvellous news.

Thank you very much. Goodbye.' She put the receiver down and beamed at the girls.

'That was the police,' she told them. 'They've caught the man who broke in here. He was caught trying to sell your grandad's old watch. You know, the gold one with the inscription on it. The police circulated my list of stolen items to all the local shops that deal in that sort of thing, and one of the shopkeepers recognised it. He managed to keep the man there while he contacted the police. He's been renting a room over on the other side of town. They've already been there.' Mrs Hayes's smile widened ever more. 'And they say they found most of our things intact. Isn't that wonderful news?'

She smiled at Holly and Belinda, slightly puzzled by the blank expressions on their faces.

It seemed that Holly's theory had been shot down almost before it had got off the ground.

9 An encounter with the police

'Well, well,' said Mr Adams, sitting at the breakfast table with the *Express* in his hands. 'It looks like the police are going to have to pull their socks up.'

The previous evening Holly had told her parents about the capture of the burglar. They had been pleased and relieved to hear the news. 'I'll sleep easier knowing he's behind bars at last,' her mother had said. And that had seemed to be the end of it.

Until Holly's father came in the next morning with the newspaper.

'Now what?' Mrs Adams asked.

'Another burglary,' said Mr Adams. 'Last night. It's in the "Stop Press" here. Another break-in in MacGonnagal Street. That's up near Belinda again, isn't it?' He looked at Holly. 'Looks like that fellow they picked up isn't the only light-fingered person around here.' He folded the newspaper and started on his breakfast. 'Well, one thing's for sure. He couldn't have done last night's job. Not unless they let him out especially.'

Holly took the newspaper with her to school to show Belinda.

'Two lots of burglars?' said Belinda in disbelief.

'It looks like it,' said Holly. She shook her head. 'So I could still be right about the Greenaways.'

'I asked my mother about the keys,' said Belinda. 'I was wrong about her taking them upstairs with her. They were in her handbag. The handbag that was stolen.' She glanced past Holly. 'Here comes Tracy,' she said. 'I wouldn't mention your theory to her, if I were you. Not unless you want another row.'

'Hi, you guys,' said Tracy. 'Did you come up with anything last night?'

Holly shrugged. 'Not really.'

Tracy laughed. 'I didn't think you'd get any-where without me there to help,' she said.

'How did the juggling go?' asked Belinda.

'Don't talk to me about it,' said Tracy. 'It's a nightmare. I may just have to stand there and wave, after all. I want to go find Mark. I'll see you later.'

Holly bit back the desire to tell Tracy about her confrontation with Mark the previous day. She wanted to get things clearer in her head before she said anything more about the Greenaway family.

It was lunch-time. Holly had found herself a sunny place out of doors and was sitting with her back to

114

the school wall, the Mystery Club notebook open in her lap.

The grass area between the school building and the tennis courts was strewn with groups of students enjoying themselves. Round the back of the school games of football were being played. But out where Holly was sitting, it was peaceful and quiet.

Which gave her the perfect opportunity to ponder over some things that were puzzling her.

Her theory about the Greenaways being linked to the burglaries was, as Belinda had said, very neat. But the fact that the police had caught the man who had burgled the Hayeses' house seemed to have pulled the rug out from under it. Holly's last hope had been that the burglar would prove to be Joe Sharpe. It hadn't.

But the latest burglary definitely meant that there was someone else at work in Willow Dale. Some one, or some *ones*.

Holly chewed the end of her pen. She wondered where Belinda had got to. Belinda's first move at lunch-time was always to head for the canteen. But even with her appetite she should have been out by now.

Holly wrote the name 'Mark Greenaway' in the notebook and studied it, the end of her pen back in her mouth. The notebook was open to the burglary page. She began to jot down the things about Mark and his family that she wasn't happy about.

1. Story about living in Kensington unconvincing.
2. Cheated people out of money.
3. Lied about Joe Sharpe. Family knew about him before the faith healing meeting.
4. At least three of the houses burgled were visited by the Greenaways. What about the keys? Is this a coincidence?

She took the pen out of her mouth and poised it above the page.

'Is that my name I see there?' Mark's voice took her completely by surprise.

Holly slapped the book closed. Mark was leaning on the wall, looking down at her with a cold, hard expression in his eyes. He must have walked alongside the wall, coming quietly up to her while she had been staring at the notebook. She had no idea how long he had been there, or how much he had seen of what she had written in the book.

'It's just a diary,' Holly said as evenly as she could manage.

'Some people might object to having their names in other people's diaries,' said Mark. 'Some people might suggest that certain people should keep their noses out of other people's business.' He smiled coldly. 'Some people might get themselves into trouble with their long noses.'

Holly stood up. 'Some people shouldn't creep up and read over other people's shoulders,' she said without missing a beat.

Mark's mouth tightened to a thin line as he tried to outstare her. But Holly gazed steadily back into his eyes until eventually he had to look away.

'Miss Baker sent me to look for you,' he said. 'She wants you to try out the camcorder. She's waiting for you now.' Mark turned on his heel and walked off across the grass.

Holly looked anxiously after him, wondering how much he had read in the notebook, and, more disturbingly, what he might do about it.

Holly went into the school to find Miss Baker.

She was waiting in her form room with Steffie Smith.

'Do you want me to show you how this thing works or not?' said Steffie impatiently. 'I don't want to waste the whole of my lunch hour.'

It was no more than ten minutes' work for Holly to get the hang of the camcorder. Virtually all she had to do was rest it on a shoulder, push a button, and let modern technology take over.

Holly walked round the classroom, getting used to navigating through one eye applied to the view-finder. It was odd at first to find the whole room compacted into a tiny glass ring and she found herself stumbling over things until she got used to it.

Steffie showed her the zoom lens, used to bring things closer. Holly zoomed until Miss Baker's face grew to fill the lens.

'I think we'll put the camcorder away some-where safe now,' said Miss Baker. 'If you're happy with it.'

As she went to look for Belinda, Holly heard Tracy's voice coming from an adjacent classroom.

'I really can't do this,' she heard.

'It's simple. All it needs is practice.' That was Mark's voice.

Holly glanced through the glass panel in the door. Mark was trying to teach Tracy to juggle three coloured balls. But as Holly looked in, the balls were bouncing out of control all over the floor.

'It's no good,' said Tracy. 'I'll never be able to do it.'

'Of course you will,' said Mark. 'If my mother can do it, I'm sure you can. Now, just hold them the way I showed you.'

Holly didn't make her presence known.

As she was walking down the school steps she saw Belinda coming in through the front gates. They met out on the path.

'Where have you been?' asked Holly.

'Out investigating,' said Belinda.

'Without me?' said Holly. 'What sort of investi-gating?'

'I couldn't find you,' said Belinda. 'And there

118

wasn't time to search if I was going to get it done and get back here before the bell. I went over to the Coopers' house. I had a word with Matthew's gran.' Belinda's eyes shone. 'I've found out something very, very interesting. Apparently Mary Greenaway has this little piece of business she likes to go through when she sees people on a one-to-one basis. She likes to hold something made of metal owned by the person she's going to heal. She said it helps with the vibrations, or something like that. Have a guess at what it was that she held that belonged to old Granny Cooper?'

'I don't know,' said Holly. 'A pen?'

'No, dummy,' said Belinda. 'Keys.'

Holly's mouth fell open.

'See?' said Belinda. 'There's your link. Now if we can find out which houses Mary Greenaway has visited – and whether she always does this thing with the keys – well, that's your theory right back on the rails.'

'Except that your place was burgled by someone else,' said Holly.

'Yes,' said Belinda. 'And I've been thinking about that as well. If that business with the Great Mysterioso and my key was the same as Mary Greenaway and Granny Cooper's key, they might well have been *planning* on doing my place over. Do you see what I mean? They might have been intending to burgle my place, but got beaten to it by someone else.'

Holly didn't manage to give much attention to her lessons that afternoon. It was maddening to feel she was *that* close to making her theory work, but that the final piece of the jigsaw was eluding her. How was it possible for the Greenaways, after holding a key for only a few seconds, to walk off with a duplicate?

She met up with Belinda in the locker room at the end of school.

'Come up with anything?' asked Belinda.

Holly shook her head. She frowned as she looked at her locker. There was an envelope taped to the front. Puzzled, she peeled it off and opened it. There was a slip of paper inside. She read it.

'"If you really want to know about the burglaries, be at Oakleaves in Dorrit Road at eight tonight."'

The two friends looked at each other.

'Someone's playing games with us,' said Belinda.

Holly frowned, nibbling thoughtfully at her bottom lip. 'This is from Mark Greenaway, I'm sure of it,' she said. She looked at Belinda. 'The question is, why?'

'It's another one of his tricks,' said Belinda. 'You can bet on that.'

'I'm not so sure,' said Holly. She told Belinda about her encounter with Mark that lunch-time.

120

'He must have seen that I'd written "Burglaries" at the top of the page,' she said. 'Perhaps he wants to meet me somewhere private to convince me he's not involved. Do you know Oakleaves?'

'Yes,' said Belinda. 'It's an old place right on the top of the hill. It's a nursing home. Why would he choose there, I wonder?'

'I don't know,' said Holly, pulling her bag out of her locker and slinging it over her shoulder. 'But I intend to find out.'

Belinda stared at her. 'You're not seriously considering going, are you?'

'Of course. If Mark's got something he wants to tell me, then I intend to hear it.'

Belinda shook her head. 'It'll be a pack of lies, whatever he says,' she said. 'If he told me the sun was shining I'd have to go outside and check before I believed it.'

Holly shrugged. 'I'll let you know,' she said.

'Oh, no you won't,' Belinda said vehemently. 'I'm coming with you.'

The huge, rambling house known as the Oakleaves Nursing Home stood alone on the crest of the hill, its expansive lawns dotted with trees and surrounded by a high brick wall.

It was ten minutes to eight as the two girls looked in through the wrought-iron gates.

'I do hope this is a good idea,' said Belinda.

'I still think we're crazy to have come here at all.'

Holly pushed the gate open and scanned the grounds. There were two or three cars parked over by the building, but other than that the place was quiet and deserted.

'Where should we wait, do you think?' asked Belinda.

'I don't know. Near the gates, I suppose,' said Holly.

'Look,' said Belinda. 'I know you're determined to go through with this despite anything I say, but I really think it would make sense for us to keep out of sight until we know exactly what's going on. I mean, supposing it is Mark and he brings along some heavies to rough us up? He might, you know, if he has got something to do with those burglaries and he thinks we're on to him.'

The thought had already crossed Holly's mind. 'I don't think so,' she said. 'That would only prove he was involved. No, I think he's concocted some plausible story to convince us he's innocent. But it wouldn't do any harm to keep out of sight, all the same.'

It was easy enough to find a shaded spot in amongst the trees where they could wait, out of view but in full sight of the gates.

They waited.

Belinda looked at her watch. Eight o'clock had

come and gone without a single person entering the gates. A few lights went on in the building. Belinda shifted from foot to foot.

'He's not coming,' she said. 'I bet this was what he had planned all along. To get you here and leave you standing around like a dummy half the evening. He's probably at home at this very moment, laughing his head off.'

They heard footsteps out on the pavement, and muffled voices.

Holly gripped Belinda's wrist.

'He's brought some other people with him,' she whispered.

'I think we're in trouble,' murmured Belinda. 'I *knew* this was a mad idea.'

The two girls backed deeper into the trees, waiting with hammering hearts for the owners of the voices to appear. Holly wished with all her heart that she had listened to Belinda and ignored the note.

Holly let out a gasp of relief as two middle-aged men walked straight past the gates and vanished along the pavement.

'We're getting too jumpy,' she said. 'You're right. He's not coming. We might as well go.'

They were about to emerge from the shelter of the trees when they heard a car draw up outside the gates.

They looked questioningly at each other.

A car door opened, accompanied by a curious, distorted, buzzing voice.

'What's that?' said Belinda.

'I'm not sure,' said Holly. 'It sounds like . . . oh!'

A policeman and a policewoman stood at the gates. The two girls exchanged puzzled glances.

The police officers walked through the gates, their heads turning as they looked around.

'There!' The policewoman spotted the two girls and pointed.

Holly and Belinda came out from under the trees.

'What are you doing here?' asked the policeman.

'Waiting for a friend,' said Holly.

His eyes narrowed. 'This is private property. We've had a call about people acting suspiciously up here. Do you know anything about it?'

'We haven't seen anyone,' said Belinda. 'And we've been here ages.'

The policeman looked curiously at them. 'Do you often spend your time hanging about on private property waiting for *friends*?'

'No,' mumbled Belinda. 'Not often.'

The policewoman headed over to the big house while the man spoke into the radio attached to his collar.

'Looks like a false alarm,' he said. 'It's just a

couple of kids. A couple of girls.' A buzzing, crackling voice sounded over the radio. It was amazing that the man could understand what was being said. 'OK,' he replied. He looked at the two girls, taking a notebook out of his breast pocket.

'Right,' he said. 'We'll have your names and addresses, I think. Just in case we need to follow this up.'

The policewoman came back. 'They don't know anything about it in there,' she said. 'The phone call didn't come from the house.'

The policeman gave the two girls a hard look.

'We haven't done anything,' said Holly. 'We were only waiting for someone. We'd arranged to meet here, but . . . '

'But?' said the policeman.

'He didn't turn up,' said Holly weakly. She looked at Belinda. 'Perhaps we'd better go,' she said.

'Perhaps you'd better,' said the policewoman. 'And if this friend of yours has got anything to do with the call we got at the station, I think you'd do well to inform him that wasting police time is a serious offence.'

The two officers escorted Holly and Belinda out.

'Stupid kids,' they heard the man say as they got back into the squad car.

They watched in silence as the car drew away.

Belinda breathed a sigh of relief.

'I suppose that's what he had planned all along,' said Holly. 'To get us here, then call the police.'

'The rat!' said Belinda. 'We could have got into serious trouble.'

'Not half so serious as the trouble he's going to be in tomorrow when I get my hands on him,' said Holly.

They set off for home.

Mark Greenaway obviously thought he could make a fool of her. Holly was determined to prove that he was wrong.

10   Tricking a trickster

'Tracy? Have you seen Mark?'

Tracy was in her classroom early the next morning, vainly trying to get the three coloured juggling balls to behave in her floundering hands. She looked round in surprise at the sound of Holly's angry voice.

'No, not this morning,' said Tracy. 'Why?'

A sleepless night had not improved Holly's temper. She had lain awake, getting angrier by the minute. It was Mark Greenaway's conceit, more than anything else, that infuriated her. The idea he seemed to have that he could get away with anything. Cheating people out of money with his card tricks. Lying, and then trying to cover up the lies with yet more lies.

And then setting her and Belinda up like that. Sending them off on a wild goose chase. Phoning the police. Obviously hoping they would get into trouble.

'I want to talk to him,' said Holly. 'He's got some explaining to do.'

'What now?' asked Tracy. 'I thought we'd agreed that you'd leave him alone.'

'I know,' said Holly. 'But you don't know the half of what's been going on. It's not just the lies anymore, Tracy. There are things we haven't told you.'

Tracy gave her a puzzled look. 'Like what?'

'Yes,' said Mark's voice from behind Holly. 'Like what?'

Holly spun round. Mark was standing in the doorway. His face broke into a broad smile.

'You set us up last night,' stormed Holly. 'You deliberately got us to go to Oakleaves and then called the police.'

'I don't know what you're talking about,' said Mark. 'I was at home watching television last night.'

'What *is* this?' demanded Tracy.

In a flurry of angry words, Holly told her about the bogus note and their encounter with the police. 'It was him,' she said, pointing at Mark. 'Trying to get us into trouble.'

'Why should I do that?' Mark said smoothly. 'I didn't leave you any notes.' His face was the picture of innocence. 'Truly,' he said. 'You've got the wrong person.'

'Holly, why *would* Mark do that?' asked Tracy.

'Because he saw something about the burglaries in our notebook, and he saw his name written there,' said Holly.

Tracy stared dumbfounded at her. 'You think Mark has got something to do with those burglaries?' she gasped.

Holly hadn't intended to tell Tracy about her suspicions, at least not until she had enough proof to convince her.

'You see?' Mark said to Tracy. 'You see how crazy that pair is? They haven't liked me from the start, and now they're trying to turn you against me as well. That's all this is – spite. I've got nothing to do with any burglaries. You believe me, don't you, Tracy?'

'Of course I do,' said Tracy. She turned to Holly. 'How could you?' she said. 'How could you behave like this?'

'Tracy, it isn't like that at all . . . ' began Holly.

'I don't want to hear any more,' said Tracy. Without another word she walked out of the classroom, slamming the door as she went.

Holly gave Mark a cold look. 'You don't fool me,' she said.

Mark smiled. 'Don't I? Who was it left standing around for the police last night?'

'So you admit it was you who left the note?' said Holly.

'Yes, it was me,' he said. 'I thought it was about time you were taught to mind your own business. I don't like being accused of things I haven't done.'

'I haven't accused you of anything,' said Holly.

'I'm not blind,' said Mark. 'I saw what you had written in that book of yours.' He glowered at her. 'You're lucky you didn't get worse,' he said. 'I know some people who would have given you a really bad time over something like that. If you take my advice, you'll mind your own business from now on.'

'Is that a threat, Mark?' Holly said evenly.

Mark smiled grimly. 'Why should I need to threaten you? I haven't done anything, so there's nothing for you to find out. You keep on playing your amateur detective games if it amuses you. Just leave me and Tracy alone, that's all I'm saying. Keep your nose out.'

As he opened the door to leave, Belinda almost bumped into him.

'And *you'd* better watch your step as well,' said Mark, storming away.

'Why?' called Belinda after him. 'Worried I might tread on your toes?' She came into the classroom. 'What was all that about?' she asked.

Holly told her what had happened.

Belinda sat on a desk, her forehead wrinkled. 'He's got a point, though, hasn't he?' she said. 'There's really nothing to link the Greenaways to the burglaries. Not unless we can come up with something a bit more convincing about the keys.'

'I know,' said Holly. 'And maybe I am wrong. But I just feel so *sure* about it.'

'I think,' Belinda said slowly, 'that either we should go to the police and tell them about your theory with the keys, or . . .' She looked across at Holly. 'Or we should drop the whole thing.'

Holly sighed. 'Do you think the police would believe us after last night? Our evidence is pretty thin, to say the least. They'd just think the same as Tracy does – that we've got some stupid vendetta going against Mark.'

'So?' said Belinda. 'What's the plan?'

'I don't know,' said Holly. 'I really don't know.'

'What's wrong with you this evening?' Holly's mother looked up from the book she was reading. 'You've been wandering around like a lost soul for the last two hours.'

'Nothing,' said Holly. She was standing staring out of the living-room window.

The truth was that she was feeling very down. A day ago she had thought she was hot on the trail of the burglars, but now she felt as if it had all been a waste of time. Belinda was right – there was nothing they could do. Holly wasn't used to hitting up against a brick wall like this. In the past the Mystery Club had always come through.

But in the past it had always been the three of them. Holly, Belinda and Tracy. The Mystery Club. But since the appearance of Mark Greenaway in

Willow Dale the Mystery Club seemed to have fallen apart.

Holly's only hope now was that the trouble between them and Tracy would blow over and that they would be able to get back together again like the old days. But Holly wasn't very hopeful. It felt as if things would never be the same while Mark Greenaway was still in the picture.

'If you're at a loose end,' said her mother, 'you could always go and help Jamie.'

Jamie had been given the run of the spare bedroom to make his plaster gnomes. The room was empty and uncarpeted, so he could make all the mess he liked.

Holly went upstairs and, for want of anything better to do with herself, looked in on Jamie.

Practice with the plaster of Paris mixture hadn't resulted in Jamie making any less mess. But he had finally, with some help from his father, got the knack of adding the right amount of water to the white powder and getting it into the rubbery moulds without spilling most of it over himself.

He was working at a wallpapering table, using an old saucepan to mix the plaster in.

As Holly looked in, he was busily painting bright red hats on to a row of quite respectable-looking gnomes.

'They look good,' said Holly.

'Don't touch,' said Jamie. 'They're wet.'

'I can see that,' said Holly. 'Have you nearly finished, or what? Is there anything I can do?'

'There are two more in the moulds and then that's the lot,' said Jamie, a hint of pride in his voice. 'But you could give me a hand with the painting.'

'What's this?' Holly pointed to a funny looking blob of leftover plaster on the table.

'It's my hand print,' said Jamie. 'See? If you let the stuff go sort of half-set it gets like Plasticine and you can make prints in it.'

Holly looked more closely. Clearly sunken into the hardening lump of plaster was the impression of a hand.

'It was Dad's idea,' said Jamie. 'He said I should keep it safe somewhere, and then in a few years I could see how much bigger my hand had got. Great, eh?'

'Great,' said Holly, not very impressed. 'You should do one of your head – see if your brain grows at all.'

'I'll do one of your nose if you like,' said Jamie.

'No, thanks, I – ' She stopped, staring at the indented piece of plaster. 'What did you say just then?'

'I said I could do a print of your nose,' said Jamie.

'No. Before that. You said when it begins to set it gets like Plasticine,' said Holly.

'Yes, it does. So?'

'Jamie!' yelled Holly. 'You're brilliant!' She leaned across the table, grabbing his head and planting a kiss on his dusty forehead.

'Get off me,' he said, squirming out from between her hands. 'Have you gone potty or something?'

'No. No. I haven't gone potty at all. But I've *got* it, Jamie. I've figured out how they did it!' Holly said excitedly. 'Plasticine!'

'How who did what?' said Jamie. 'Mind my gnomes, will you. What are you going on about?'

'Never mind,' said Holly. 'I've got to phone Belinda.'

Jamie stared after her as she rushed out of the room.

'Thanks for all your help,' he called. 'I couldn't have managed without you.'

But Holly was too thrilled with her discovery even to hear what he had said.

Belinda was in her bedroom when Holly rang. She was watching television and eating chocolate-coated peanuts.

Holly's voice was so excited that it was difficult for Belinda to understand what she was saying.

'Holly,' she said into the phone. 'Slow down, will you? I can't keep up with you.'

'I've got it!' shouted Holly. 'I know how it was done!'

'How what was done?' Belinda asked blankly.

A scream of exasperation echoed down the receiver. 'The burglaries!' yelled Holly. 'Look, meet me at the corner of Tracy's street. We can tell her now. We can tell her everything about it!'

Belinda listened with her mouth hanging open as Holly explained about the Plasticine.

'Right,' said Belinda. 'Give me half an hour to get there.'

Holly was already waiting for her as she came to the corner of the street where Tracy and her mother lived.

'I've got a plan,' said Holly. She explained her idea to Belinda as they walked along to Tracy's terraced house.

Mrs Foster answered the door. She seemed surprised to see them.

'Hello, Holly, Belinda,' she said, giving them a curious look.

'Is Tracy in?' asked Holly.

'Yes, she's upstairs.' Mrs Foster opened the door and they went into the hall. 'I thought you'd had a falling-out,' she said. 'Tracy said you weren't talking. She seemed quite upset about it.'

'We've come to make up,' said Belinda.

The look that Tracy gave them as they walked into her room was not very promising.

She was standing in the middle of the carpet, staring down at three coloured balls that lay scattered on the floor. As she looked up, her annoyed frown deepened.

'We need to talk,' said Holly.

'I'm kind of busy right now,' said Tracy.

'Please?' said Holly. 'Just give us five minutes. And then, if you say so, we'll go.'

'I guess I can give you five minutes,' said Tracy. 'But if it's about Mark . . . '

'Just *listen*, will you?' said Belinda.

'OK,' said Tracy. 'I'm listening.'

It wasn't easy for Holly to unravel the tale of their suspicions under Tracy's disbelieving eyes. 'The one thing we couldn't figure out,' said Holly, 'was how they could have got duplicates of the keys. But I think I've got that now. Can I show you?'

'Go ahead,' said Tracy.

'OK. Give me your door key,' said Holly. Tracy reached into her jeans pocket and pulled out a small bunch of keys. Holly took them from her.

'How's the juggling coming along?' asked Belinda.

'Huh?' Tracy looked at Belinda, then at the coloured balls on the floor. 'Not very well,' she said. 'I'm practising like crazy, but I can't seem to get it together at all.' She looked suspiciously at Holly. 'What is all this?'

'Here are your keys back,' said Holly.

Tracy took her keys. 'So?' she said. 'What's the big deal here?'

'I've made a copy of your front door key,' said

136

Holly. She held her hand out. Hidden in her palm was a wad of Plasticine. Clearly indented on the Plasticine was the outline of Tracy's key.

'Get it?' said Belinda. 'While I distracted your attention Holly made the copy. That's what we think Mary Greenaway has been doing. She asks to hold something metal when she goes to people's houses. She says it helps with the vibrations – you know, helps her cure people. And the Great Mysterioso had my keys at that party, remember?'

'Yes, but hold on,' said Tracy. 'The police *found* the guy who did your place over.'

'I know,' said Belinda. 'But we're pretty sure that the Greenaways *intended* to burgle us. If we're right, they've got a copy of my key – but they haven't used it yet.'

'*If* you're right,' said Tracy. 'That's a pretty big if.' But the certainty had gone out of her voice. Something in Holly's explanation had clearly shaken her belief in Mark. 'Shouldn't you tell the police about this?' she said.

'I think we can do better than that,' said Holly. 'But we'll need your help. We want to set a trap for them.'

'I don't know,' said Tracy. 'I can't believe Mark is involved in all this. I know his mom's kind of weird – and that business with the guy at the shop sounds pretty kooky. I mean, you must be right – if the guy was getting letters sent to him there, they

137

must have known him all along. But *this*? Come on, you guys, this is something else!'

'If he's innocent the trap won't work,' said Holly. 'It's as simple as that.'

'I'm not happy about setting him up,' said Tracy. 'He trusts me.'

'That's why we need your help,' said Belinda. 'Because he trusts you. Right now, he thinks we're not talking to each other, so he won't dream that you're involved in anything we've got planned.'

Tracy winced at this. 'I really don't know,' she said. 'I'm supposed to be his friend. He's never done me any harm – it's you guys he doesn't like. And that's only because of what he saw you'd written in the notebook.'

'We've always been through these things together in the past,' said Holly. 'And we really do need your help.'

Tracy gave them a troubled look. 'OK,' she said. 'I'll do it, if you're so certain you're right. What do you want me to do?'

'It's simple,' said Holly. 'All you need to do is let it slip that Belinda's house is going to be empty on Friday night. Just mention to Mark in passing that Belinda and her mum are staying with relatives for the night, and that there won't be anyone there.'

'Don't make a big thing of it,' said Belinda. 'You could just say it to someone else while he's listening.'

'And then what?' asked Tracy.

'And then,' said Holly, her eyes gleaming. 'I stay at Belinda's on Friday night. We keep our eyes and ears open and if we hear anyone prowling about . . .'

'We nab them!' said Belinda. 'One quick phone call to the police from the extension in my bedroom and they're caught red-handed.'

'And your mother is up for that?' Tracy asked incredulously.

'That's the best part of it,' said Belinda. 'My mother *is* going to be away on Friday night. She's visiting my Aunt Susie on Friday, and she always stayed the night. We'll have the place to ourselves.' She grinned at Tracy. 'Just us, the burglars and half a dozen heavy-footed policemen.'

'OK,' said Tracy. 'I'll do it. But I want to be there on Friday night. I want to be there when it happens.' She gave them an uncertain look. '*If* it happens.'

'It'll happen,' said Holly. 'I'm sure of it.'

11 *The trap is set*

It was Friday afternoon. The Willow Dale Festival was only one day away. Excitement and anticipation were running through the school like electricity. It was one of those afternoons when teachers found it difficult to get anyone to pay attention in class.

Every now and then throughout the day, Holly had spotted Tracy. They would exchange a glance, and Tracy would shake her head, meaning she hadn't yet the chance to set the trap.

In theory it was a simple enough thing to do. All that was required was that Tracy should casually mention, in Mark's hearing, that Belinda and her mother would be out of town that night, and that the house would be empty.

Turning that theory into practice proved a lot more frustrating than Tracy had anticipated. The problem was to make her comment sound *casual*. If Mark suspected for a moment that a trap was being set, then Holly's plan would fall to pieces.

At the end of school Holly and Belinda met in the girls' locker room.

'Have you seen Tracy?' asked Belinda. 'Has she done it yet?'

'I haven't seen her since the first lesson after lunch,' said Holly. 'And she hadn't managed it then.'

'I'm going to end up a nervous wreck,' said Belinda. 'What's she playing at?'

Holly looked around the busy locker room. 'I thought we might see her here,' she said. 'We can't go looking for her. We're not supposed to be talking to her.'

Belinda shook her head gloomily. 'It's not going to work,' she said. 'I knew it all along.'

Holly hitched her bag on to her shoulder. 'There's still time,' she said hopefully.

Belinda snorted. 'It's never any good giving Tracy something complicated to do,' she said. She looked at Holly and grinned, knowing she was being unfair. 'Perhaps we should send him a written invitation! "Dear Mark, the Hayes household will be empty tonight. Would the last burglar to leave please remember to switch off the lights."'

As they came out of the main entrance, they found Jamie sitting on the steps. He was obviously waiting for Holly. He jumped up as he saw her.

'Where did you say that shop was?' he asked. 'You know – the one you got those tricks from?'

'Radnor Street,' said Holly. 'Why?'

'I want to go and get some more. Those rubber sweets are brilliant. You should have seen my mate Philip's face when he tried to eat one,' said Jamie. He mimed the surprise as teeth came down on a plastic chocolate. 'It was a scream,' he said. 'Whereabouts is Radnor Street?'

Holly began explaining, but stopped when she saw a blank look come over Jamie's face.

'I'll never remember all that,' he said.

'I can draw you a map,' said Holly.

'Couldn't you just *show* me?' said Jamie.

'I've got better things to do than take you into town,' said Holly. 'All you've got to do is get the bus at – '

'I haven't got any money for bus fares,' said Jamie.

'Then how did you intend paying for anything?' asked Holly.

Jamie put on his most endearing smile.

'Oh, I get it,' said Holly. 'I'm supposed to lend you some money, am I?'

'Just until I get my allowance,' said Jamie. 'You know you're my favourite sister of all time, don't you? The best sister in the world?'

'No, I'm not,' said Holly. 'I'm the *worst* sister in the world. You said so a couple of days ago.'

'I'll come with you, if you like,' said Belinda.

She gave Holly a conspiratorial look. 'We could have another look in the shop while we are there, couldn't we? You never know, we might see something *interesting*.'

'OK,' said Holly. 'Let's go. But I'm not lending you all my money, pest.'

They were almost out of the gates when they heard running feet behind them. It was Tracy.

'I've done it,' she said breathlessly. 'You wouldn't believe how difficult it was to get it in a conversation. In the end it was Steffie Smith who helped. She was moaning about having to get up early tomorrow for the festival and I said it'll be even worse for Belinda – she can hardly drag herself out of bed at the best of times – and tomorrow morning she'll have to come in all the way from Thurston, because she and her mom are staying over there tonight.' Tracy grinned. 'Brilliant or what?'

'What do you mean, I have trouble dragging myself out of bed?' said Belinda.

Tracy waved a dismissive hand. 'Never mind about that,' she said. 'The point is, I think it worked. Mark definitely heard me.'

'What's going on?' asked Jamie.

'Nothing,' said Holly. 'Just girl-talk.' She nodded at Tracy. 'See you at Belinda's at about half-seven then?'

'I'll be there,' said Tracy.

143

'I thought you told Mum this morning that you were stopping over at Belinda's tonight?' said Jamie.

'I am,' said Holly.

'But Tracy just said Belinda was going to be somewhere else,' said Jamie.

'Look.' Holly frowned at him. 'Will you just mind your own business please, Jamie?'

'Pardon me for breathing,' said Jamie. 'Can we get off now? I've got to be back here in an hour for football practice.'

They said goodbye to Tracy, and Holly, Belinda and Jamie caught the bus into town.

'How much spare money have you got?' Jamie asked Holly.

'I don't have any *spare* money at all,' said Holly. 'But I can probably find a bit to lend you.'

'How much? I'd like to get a whole bag of tricks.'

'We'll see when we get there,' said Holly.

As it turned out, Jamie was saved the bother of turning on his charm. The shop was closed.

Jamie peered through the door into the unlit interior. There on the revolving rack, tantalisingly out of reach, were the suspended packs of tricks.

'It should be open,' he said. 'Look, it says nine to six.'

144

'Well, it isn't,' said Holly. 'So hard luck.'

Jamie pushed his hands into his pockets. 'Rotten lot,' he said. 'I might as well get back to school, then.'

'Does Mum know you're playing football this evening?' asked Holly.

Jamie nodded morosely. Pausing only to cadge the return bus fare from Holly, he headed for the bus stop, leaving the two girls standing outside the shop.

'I don't suppose there's anyone in there?' said Belinda, looking in through the window.

'It doesn't look like it,' said Holly.

'We could always have a sneaky look round the back,' said Belinda. 'You never know – we might spot something.'

'Like what?' said Holly. 'Huge bags with "swag" written on them?'

'You're getting very sarcastic,' said Belinda. 'I can't think where you've picked that up from.'

'From you, mostly,' said Holly. 'Come on then. Let's have a quick look.'

They went to the side of the shop and walked down the narrow alley. High walls reared up on either side of them. Dark, neglected walls punctuated with grimy windows, blinded by years of encrusted dirt.

A wooden fence, about six feet high, enclosed a small backyard or garden. It led down a slight slope to an alley that ran along the back of the entire row. There was a tall gate in the fence at the bottom. Holly tried the rusty handle but it wouldn't move. She looked at the dark red grit that came off on her hand.

Belinda looked both ways along the deserted alley.

'I wish Tracy was here,' she said. 'She could be up and over that wall in a couple of seconds.'

Holly pointed to an old iron dustbin, standing forlornly by the fence, half-eaten away by rust. 'If you hold me steady, I'll climb up on the lid and have a look over,' she said.

The dustbin creaked and groaned as Holly clambered up.

She found herself looking down into a tangle of weeds and rubbish. Broken crates lay amongst heaps of old plastic sheeting and bundles of sodden newspapers. The back door of the shop was closed, but there was a window next to it through which Holly could vaguely see into a back room. She was ready to duck out of sight at the first hint that anyone was at home, but the place seemed lifeless.

'Anything?' asked Belinda.

'Not really,' said Holly. The crates piled against the fence looked as though they would carry her weight. 'I'm going to climb over,' she said. 'There's no curtain on the back window. I might be able to see something. Keep watch.'

She hooked a foot over the top of the fence and rolled herself over and on to the crates. They rocked and settled, but remained firm.

'Careful,' called Belinda as her friend disappeared from sight.

'I'm OK,' Holly's voice came back.

Belinda went back up the alley, keeping in the shadows, but able to see comings and going in the main street.

Meanwhile Holly picked her way across the obstacle course of the backyard. Cautiously, she slid an eye round the corner of the filthy window.

It was a dark room with a naked light bulb hanging from the ceiling. Not the sort of room anyone would live in, just an old stockroom heaped with boxes. There was a table hard up against the window, with things lying on the surface.

Holly frowned, rubbing at the glass to try and clear a ring in the dirt. She recognised one of the things. It was a bench-top vice. Lying beside it were a number of files. The sort her father used for filing metal, except that these were much smaller and thinner.

Holly's eyes widened. There was a metal box on the table. A box half-filled with keys.

A vice. Files. A box of keys. A vice to hold the keys in, and files to shape the keys.

Holly's heart beat loudly. This was *it*! This was where they made the copy keys that they used to get into people's houses!

Belinda bit nervously at her nails, glancing frequently back down the alley. She hoped that Holly would hurry up and reappear round the bottom of the fence.

It was as she turned from one of these anxious looks that her heart nearly cracked her ribs with shock. Joe Sharpe was crossing the road. He was heading for the shop.

Belinda shrank into the shadows, praying that he wouldn't look down the alley, praying that he wouldn't spot her.

She was in luck.

Joe Sharpe's face was drawn with concentration. He was reading a tightly folded newspaper as he walked along. But he was definitely walking straight towards the front of the shop. As he reached the pavement, Belinda saw him feel in his pocket and draw out a bunch of keys.

He was going to open the shop.

The moment he was out of sight, Belinda pelted back down the alley. She had to warn Holly.

The dustbin shook and rattled as she clambered up on to it. There was a terrible moment as the lid suddenly crumpled under her weight. She grabbed at the top of the fence. The lid had caved in, but still held her. She could see Holly at the far end of the chaotic yard.

She didn't want to shout, for fear of drawing unwanted attention to herself. She waved and beat her hand on the fence.

Holly looked round, seeing the anxious look on Belinda's face and the frantic waving of her arm.

'Quick!' Belinda's voice was a loud whisper.

Holly didn't wait for explanations. She ran down the cluttered yard, jumping over broken boxes and skipping round piles of debris. Her foot skidded on a slick piece of plastic sheeting and she fell.

Belinda bit her lip, urging her friend on as she saw the light go on in the back room.

Holly scrambled up and ran to the fence, not daring to look back. She flung herself at the heaped crates and there was a crash as they fell.

Belinda saw Joe Sharpe in the back room. Her instinct was to duck out of sight, but she couldn't leave Holly stranded.

Joe Sharpe's face showed white at the window as he looked out. She saw surprise and anger blaze across his face.

Belinda leaned over the fence and caught Holly's arms as she scrambled to escape.

The face at the window vanished.

Belinda pulled back with all her strength. Holly found a foothold on the fence and came over the top with a rush, almost knocking Belinda flying.

The dustbin finally gave up the ghost and the two of them went tumbling into the dust of the alleyway.

They heard a shout and the bang of a door bursting open. They didn't wait for any more. Heedless of their scratches and bruises, the two girls ran helter-skelter along the alley, not daring to glance back or stop until they were several streets away. They found the quiet refuge of the churchyard and flung themselves, gasping, on a bench, fighting for breath.

'Do you think he recognised us?' panted Belinda.

'I hope not,' said Holly. 'I really hope not.'

Belinda and Holly arrived at Belinda's house in the early evening. There was a note from Mrs Hayes, telling her where food could be found – as if she didn't know! – and reminding her to do several things that she wouldn't have forgotten anyway. Finally, in capital letters and underlined, a reminder to lock up securely.

They talked excitedly about Holly's discovery, going over the whole thing again when Tracy arrived.

'It's the final bit of evidence,' said Holly. 'You must believe the Greenaways are involved with the burglaries now, surely?'

'I guess so,' said Tracy. 'But it still doesn't prove Mark has anything to do with it.'

Tracy was scathing when she heard of Holly's hectic escape.

'I'd have been over that wall like a jack-rabbit,' she said when they told her about the scramble and panic of their flight. 'You two are OK with the theories, but when it comes to action, you're about as good as Mickey Mouse and Donald Duck.'

She rummaged in her bag and drew out a camera. 'I thought this might come in handy,' she said. 'That way, even if we spook them and they make a run for it, we'll have a photo of them to show the police.'

They decided to make the first floor landing their base. From there they could hear the slightest sound from the front door, and Belinda could make an instant dash to the phone in her bedroom.

They sat there for a couple of hours as the night gathered round them. They didn't put any lights on. The house had to appear deserted.

'Isn't it weird how different everything looks in the dark?' said Belinda, peering down the stairs into the gloom. She looked at Holly. 'It's at moments like this that I wish you didn't have quite so many bright ideas.'

'We could tell each other stories to pass the time,' suggested Holly.

'I know some good ghost stories,' said Tracy.

'Don't you dare,' said Belinda. 'I'm feeling twitchy enough as it is.' She shivered. 'Is anyone

151

peckish? I could nip down and get us a quick snack.'

The quick snack turned into a major picnic on the carpet, and for a while they almost forgot how spooky it was, especially as Belinda had found a little candle for them to see by. But once the food was finished they found themselves sitting silently, straining their ears for any sound.

'What was that?' hissed Tracy.

'An owl,' came Belinda's tired voice.

'Are you sure?'

'Think I don't know an owl when I hear one?' said Belinda crossly.

Holly stifled a yawn. 'What's the time?' she asked.

'Just after midnight,' said Tracy. 'How long do you think we'll have to wait, you guys? I'm nodding off here.'

'Perhaps we should take it in turns to keep watch?' suggested Holly.

'I'm not sitting here on my own,' said Belinda.

'They're not coming,' said Tracy, stretching her stiff legs out. 'I told you Mark wasn't involved. Didn't I tell you?'

'Shh!' said Belinda.

'I won't shush,' said Tracy. 'I'm telling you – '

'I think I heard something,' interrupted Belinda.

The sat poised in absolute silence, hardly daring to breathe. A few suspenseful seconds ticked by.

'What do you think you heard?' asked Holly.

'A car,' whispered Belinda. She licked her fingers and doused the candle. The sudden darkness sent shivers down their spines.

'Oh, lordy . . .' murmured Tracy.

They all heard it. The sound of footsteps in the front porch. Holly crept on all fours to the head of the stairs and slid an eye round the banisters. Her breath hissed as she saw a shadow through the glass panels in the front door.

'It's them,' she whispered. 'Belinda, get to the phone. Quick!'

Tracy felt for her camera in the darkness.

They heard the chink of a key in the lock.

Tracy clicked the safety lock off her camera and crawled past Holly. She knelt at the head of the stairs, her camera ready at her eye, trying to keep it steady in her trembling hands.

The door opened and a dark figure entered the hall.

There was a sudden flare of light as Tracy pressed the shutter release and the flash illuminated the staircase and the long hall below.

In that instant of blazing white light Holly and Tracy could see exactly who it was that stood revealed in the hall.

'Belinda!' came Mrs Hayes's startled voice. 'What on earth do you think you're doing?'

Belinda slammed the phone down in mid-dial

and came running out to hang, open-mouthed, over the banisters.

'Mum?'

'Good heavens!' cried Mrs Hayes, blinking at the three faces that stared down at her in disbelief. 'What in the name of sanity are you girls playing at?'

The three friends looked at one another, then down at Mrs Hayes's wrathful face.

It seemed that their burglar trap had closed on a very unexpected quarry.

'Hello, Mum,' said Belinda hopefully. 'It's OK. Don't get mad. I can *explain*.'

Holly's head sank until her forehead was against the carpet. This was going to need quite a lot of explaining.

12 The juggler's hands

Mrs Hayes was not impressed.

'You've just given me the fright of my life,' she said. 'And now you tell me a lot of nonsense about trying to catch burglars!' She looked sternly at the three anxious faces in front of her. They had done their best to explain, but Mrs Hayes was not in the mood to listen patiently to them. Especially as they were all trying to speak at once.

'It's not nonsense,' said Belinda in a subdued voice.

'Really, it isn't,' added Holly. 'We've worked it all out.'

'If you're as certain about all of this as you say,' said Mrs Hayes, 'then it's your duty to inform the police.' Her hand strayed towards the telephone. '*Shall* I phone them?'

The three friends looked at one another.

'No,' said Belinda.

'We can't prove we're right,' said Holly. 'But we *are*. I know we are.'

Mrs Hayes gave them a tired look. 'I know you

three are always getting up to something,' she said. 'I can cope with that. What I can't and won't put up with is when your wild imaginations cause chaos in my own home. Things have gone too far when a woman can't open her own front door without being half-blinded and scared out of her wits. And what about the mess on the landing?'

'We would have cleared all that up,' said Belinda. 'You weren't supposed to be coming home.'

'Your Aunt Susie is in the middle of decorating her spare bedroom,' said Mrs Hayes. 'Which is why I didn't stay there. And I come home to find all this.' She shook her head. 'It seems fortunate that I did, if this is the sort of thing you get up to the moment my back is turned.'

'I guess we kind of goofed-up, didn't we?' said Tracy.

Mrs Hayes stared at her for a moment. 'I think you should all go to bed now,' she said quietly. 'I don't suppose I shall be able to sleep. Not after this.' She gave them a weary smile. 'I'll sit up and read for a while. Just in case your burglars *do* turn up.'

Holly and Tracy lay sleeplessly in the spare bedroom.

'This is going to make for a great entry in the notebook,' Tracy said gloomily. 'Burglar trap a dismal failure.'

Holly turned over restlessly. It was past two

o'clock but she was no more able to get off to sleep than her friend. 'I was so sure it would work,' she said. 'And now we look like complete idiots. Why didn't they come?'

'Because Mark isn't involved,' said Tracy. 'I've been telling you that all along.'

Holly didn't reply.

Half an hour later she was still churning around under the covers, consumed by embarrassment and quite certain that she wouldn't get a wink of sleep.

No matter what Tracy said, she was still unconvinced of Mark's innocence. And how could she sleep, with her ears primed for a half hoped-for and half dreaded sound of footsteps in the hall downstairs?

But eventually, at some time well towards dawn, Holly did fall asleep.

Holly woke up suddenly, realising that it was the morning of the Willow Dale Festival. They all had a full day ahead of them, and she felt like she could happily have spent another six hours in bed.

She padded downstairs. The house was cool and serene. There was no sign of a burglary. Either Mark hadn't risen to the bait, or . . . or perhaps Tracy was right about him all the time.

Tracy was relatively bright-eyed when she got up, although she didn't have the energy for her usual morning run. But it was a major task to get Belinda even to open a single eye.

'Leave me alone, go 'way,' she grumbled, pulling the duvet over her head.

'It's the festival,' said Holly, shaking her mercilessly.

'I don't care,' groaned Belinda. 'Let me sleep.'

'I'd better get off home,' said Tracy. 'I've got some things I need to pick up there. I'll see you at school.'

'OK,' said Holly. 'And I'll get Belinda up.' She looked at the grumpy lump in Belinda's bed. 'Somehow.'

Belinda finally dragged herself out of bed and stumbled downstairs.

There was no sign of Mrs Hayes at the breakfast table. Holly guessed she was upstairs, sleeping late to make up for her long night.

The two girls were heading for the front door when Mrs Hayes came down the stairs. 'I'll be along to the festival a bit later,' she told them. 'Have a good time,' she added, although there was a look in her eyes that suggested she was still very annoyed with them.

They set off for school.

It was a perfect day for the festival. The sun, in a clear blue sky, was already burning away the cool of early morning. The school car park was full and people were roaming about, making last-minute adjustments to costumes. The school float stood bright and cheerful at the gates, the light flashing on the instruments of the musicians, as they had a final practice before they set off.

'About time,' said a flustered Miss Baker, catching sight of the two girls. 'Where's that Tracy?'

'She should be here by now,' said Holly.

'She's late,' said Miss Baker. 'I knew it. I knew something disastrous was going to happen.'

'She'll be here,' said Belinda. 'Don't worry.'

Miss Baker gave them a look indicating that they didn't appreciate how much she was already worrying.

They found Jamie helping to load boxes into the back of Mr Barnard's car. Things to be sold at the charity stall.

'Do you want to see a card trick?' he asked them. 'Mark Greenaway taught it to me yesterday evening. He's not so bad when you get to know him.' Jamie pulled a pack of cards out of his back pocket and fanned them out under Holly's nose. 'Pick a card,' he said. 'Any card you like. I won't look.'

'What are you talking about?' said Holly. 'When did you see Mark?'

'He was still here when I got back yesterday for football,' said Jamie. 'I thought you'd have seen him.'

'What do you mean?' asked Holly. 'When would we have seen him?'

'He wanted to know where you lot were, so I told him you were stopping over at Belinda's house,' Jamie said unconcernedly. 'I thought he was going over there. He must have changed his mind. Do you want to see this card trick or not?'

'Jamie?' came Mr Barnard's voice. 'Are you helping, or just standing about chatting?'

Jamie didn't even notice the stunned expressions on the two girls' faces as he pocketed the cards and ran off to get another box.

'No wonder they didn't turn up,' said Belinda. 'He knew we were waiting for them all the time. Thanks to your stupid brother.'

'It's not Jamie's fault,' said Holly. 'He wasn't to know.' She stared at Belinda. 'But if Mark suspects we were setting him up, he must realise Tracy was in on it.'

'We'd better warn her,' said Belinda. 'Where on earth is she?'

Tracy still hadn't arrived, and it was getting perilously near the time for the float to head off for the rallying point where the procession was to begin.

They went into the school. Belinda changed into her jester costume and Holly collected the camcorder. Outside again they found Miss Baker getting more panicky by the minute.

'Have you any idea where she might be?' Miss Baker asked them.

'Last time we saw her she was heading off for home,' said Holly.

'OK,' said Miss Baker. 'Get in the car. I'll drive over there and pick her up.' She looked at her watch. 'We're supposed to be ready now. It's going to be a disaster. I know it is.'

It only took them five minutes to drive to Tracy's house. Holly and Belinda ran up the front path and rang the bell. Tracy's mother answered the door.

'We've come to pick Tracy up,' panted Holly. 'She's late.'

Tracy's mother gave them a bemused look. 'She's already gone,' she said. 'She was picked up ten minutes ago.'

'Picked up?' said Holly in amazement.

'That's right,' said Mrs Foster. 'That boy Mark picked her up. He was in a car with his father. Hasn't she arrived yet?'

'Not when we left,' said Belinda.

'There's a lot of traffic around today,' said Mrs Foster. 'I expect they've got themselves stuck in a jam.'

The two girls went back to Miss Baker's car.

'I don't like this,' Holly said before they got in. 'If Tracy's not at school when we get back, we've got to phone the police, right?'

They got back to the school to find the float already gone. There were still a few students standing around in the driveway.

'Has anyone seen Tracy Foster?' called Miss Baker, still unaware of Holly and Belinda's worries.

'They've gone,' said one of the boys. 'They've all gone.'

'And Tracy was with them?' asked Holly.

A girl came up. 'I saw her, Miss,' she said. 'I saw her get on to the float. She had her costume on.'

Miss Baker rested her forehead on the steering-wheel. 'Thank heavens for that,' she said. She looked round at Holly and Belinda. 'We'll catch them up,' she said. 'No problems.'

She looked at Belinda. 'You make a good jester,' she said. 'You just need one last touch.'

She took a lipstick out of her bag and painted two bright red patches on Belinda's cheeks. 'Perfect,' she said. She handed Belinda the lipstick. 'Keep it to touch your face up if it gets rubbed off.'

They drove through streets lined with bunting. The whole of the centre of the town had been cordoned off to traffic and Miss Baker had to make several detours because of police barriers.

There were people everywhere. Holly had never seen so many people in Willow Dale before. She didn't know there *were* that many people in the town.

They cruised the backstreets, looking for a parking space.

'This is hopeless,' said Miss Baker after a while.

'Look. You girls had better get out and make your way on foot. I'll join up with you as soon as I can. And you tell Tracy she's nearly given me heart-failure.'

The press of people made getting to the rallying point a slow business for the two girls. Hot-dog stalls and ice-cream vans had appeared out of nowhere. Flags hung from upstairs windows. Children ran about with balloons.

'I fancy an ice cream,' said Belinda.

'There's no time,' Holly said determinedly. 'Look! The procession has already started.'

She was right. The first floats were already making their way slowly along the street. Loud music bounced from wall to wall, mingling with the cheering and applause of the crowds. Banners fluttered merrily in the breeze and children dressed as fluffy yellow chicks were waving from the first of the floats and throwing streamers into the air.

Actors in Victorian costumes shouted and waved from the next float. 'The Willow Dale Amateur Dramatics Society', proclaimed a billowing banner.

Military music blared, and as they hung over the barrier, Holly and Belinda watched a brass band come marching up the road in perfect unison.

Belinda squirmed through the barrier and made her way to the rear of the slow-moving procession, looking for the school float. 'See you later,' she called to Holly. 'I've got to go and do my stuff.'

Holly hitched the camcorder on to her shoulder and focused on the leading float. A miniature version of a spring chicken filled the view-finder. An elbow jostled her and the fluffy chick spun out of sight.

There were too many people pushing and barging about. Holly slid out between the barriers and tried again, getting what she hoped was a good long shot of the Amateur Dramatics float as it rumbled by filled with smiling faces.

She walked to a corner and saw the whole procession strung out along the main street. She was almost deafened by the brass band. A drum-major marched at the front. Holly zoomed in on his baton as it twirled in a sparkling net of light. He flung it into the air, and the camcorder followed its rise and fall.

That was a good shot, thought Holly. *This is going to be the best video the school has ever seen*. She walked against the flow of the parade, keeping to the kerb, with her eyes to the camcorder, letting the lens slide smoothly from float to float.

In the distance, about two thirds of the way down the procession, she could see the trees on the school float. An idea struck her. She looked around and saw a waste paper bin standing beside a lamppost. Balancing carefully, she climbed on to the top of the bin, one arm round the lamppost for support, the camcorder nestling against her neck.

Yes. She could see the school float much clearer from up there. She could see Tracy in her multi-coloured costume with its gleaming sun mask, and the musicians in their costumes sitting at the back of the float. Tracy was juggling the three coloured balls like an expert, sending them high into the air and catching them without a slip. It looked as if all the practice she had done had paid off.

Holly zoomed in on the float, then let the lens slide off the back to where the younger children were dancing, and the older ones were walking along in their animal costumes and their Middle Ages costumes.

She laughed. Belinda, in her jester's costume, came dancing across the view-finder, batting people with her balloon and then cavorting off.

And then something made Holly scan the camcorder back on to the float. Back on to the gaily-coloured figure with the spinning balls.

Holly knew Tracy was athletic. She loved physical challenges. She could do things that made Holly envious. Her work-outs in the gym were strenuous enough to put Holly in bed for a week. Belinda felt tired just watching her.

But Holly had seen Tracy practising her juggling. She had seen the way the balls had taken on a rebellious life of their own, leaping out of control and bouncing uncaught around Tracy's feet.

And here she was, the balls rising and falling in

165

perfect arcs from tick-tocking hands. Never once out of control. Never a slip.

Holly pressed the zoom button, bringing the image in as close as she could. She focused on the hands, rising and opening to release the balls, falling to cup and catch. Thin hands. Thin hands with rings.

Tracy didn't wear any rings.

Holly brought the lens up to the mask. But, no, it was impossible to tell whose face was hidden under the shining golden surface, just as it was impossible to tell whose body was covered by the long colourful gown.

It isn't Tracy, thought Holly with a cold shock in her chest. *Whoever it is up there – it isn't Tracy.*

Holly pulled the zoom back, searching for Belinda.

There were no barriers along that part of the road and the edges of the crowds were ragged as the pressure of people at the back forced those in the front line off the pavement.

Holly caught sight of the jester's red balloon. Belinda had gone to the side of the road and was dancing along, bopping the onlookers with the balloon. Even as Holly was about to take her eye from the view-finder, a hand came out of the crowd and grabbed Belinda by the wrist. Holly saw it clearly – as clearly as if she had been only a few feet away rather than fifty or so metres.

The hand tugged Belinda to the side. Holly turned the camcorder slightly.

The hand belonged to Joe Sharpe. He was saying something to Belinda and Belinda was shaking her head and trying to pull her arm free.

Holly jumped down from the bin and ran towards her friend.

She ran back past the school float, her ears filled with the pounding, rhythmic music and the shouts and cheers of the crowd.

Belinda was gone.

Holly was vaguely aware of the dancers following the float, and of faces looming around her, animal faces.

She stretched to try and see above the heads of the crowd.

There! Heading away towards a side street – the bobbing globe of Belinda's balloon floated above the mass of heads.

Holly pushed forwards, trying to force her way through the crowd.

A hand grabbed her arm and pulled her backwards, away from the retreating balloon.

She turned and looked into the painted eyes of a stag mask.

A voice laughed, pulling her into the dance as she struggled to get free. 'Holly! Join in!'

'Let go. Let go!' shouted Holly.

'Don't be a misery,' laughed the voice. 'Join in.'

'Let me *go!*' Holly wrenched herself free and thrust her way, shoulder first, into the crowd. She was jostled and voices complained as she shoved her way roughly through the press.

Further away than ever, the bright red balloon waved above the mêlée.

And then Holly was through the main bulk of the crowd. Her own momentum almost made her fall. She struck up, panting against a wall and stretched for a sight of the receding balloon.

Smiling faces surrounded her. Laughing faces. Faces eating hot-dogs and candy-floss.

There was no sign of Belinda's balloon.

13 Kidnapped!

Holly gave a gasp of relief. She could see the balloon again. It was bobbing above the heads of people milling around an ice-cream van about halfway down the side street that she had just stumbled into.

She ran, zigzagging past the people in her way, her heart a thick weight in her throat, her head swimming with anxiety.

She pushed into the crowd. The small boy who held the red balloon looked at her in surprise.

It was the wrong balloon.

As Holly almost cannoned into him, the boy's hand relaxed on the string and the balloon sailed up into the sky. He let out a wail of misery.

'Sorry,' gasped Holly. 'I'm sorry. I thought . . . '

She pushed her way clear of the queue for the ice-cream van and stared around her in despair. There were balloons everywhere. Red, yellow, blue, green. Balloons with smiling faces. Silver heart-shaped balloons. A whole flock of balloons dancing in the air.

A distant flash of red caught her eye. At the far end of the street. It winked out of sight round a corner.

She ran again, oblivious of the startled faces as her feet pounded along the road. The camcorder hung heavily on its strap from her shoulder, beating against her hip, slowing her down.

She came to the corner, skidding to a halt.

Something red bobbed lazily across the pavement and came to rest. A balloon. A red balloon tied to the end of a stick.

Belinda was beginning to enjoy herself. Once she'd got over the feeling that she looked stupid in her red and white jester's outfit she started having fun, running in and out of the people following the school float, clouting them around the ears with her balloon. Banging them on the head then running off with a shriek of laughter.

The music was infectious, coaxing her feet into a half-dance as she ran and bopped with the balloon and then ran to find new victims.

She became adventurous, running along the crowds, batting their heads with her balloon like a small child running a stick along railings.

The hand that came suddenly out of the crowd and caught hold of her wrist took her too much by surprise for her even to be frightened. It was

170

not until she saw whose hand it was that she registered alarm.

'Mark wants to talk to you,' hissed Joe Sharpe. He cocked his head. 'He's been hurt. He needs to talk to you. It's about Tracy.'

'About Tracy?' said Belinda, glancing round at the receding float. 'What about Tracy?'

'Come with me,' said Joe Sharpe, tugging insistently at her. She shook her head. The cold fingers burrowed into her wrist. 'Come with me if you want to help.'

'OK, I'll come . . . but . . . ' She was almost tipped off her feet as Joe Sharpe drew her into the crowd. Before the bodies closed round her she caught a glimpse of Holly running in their direction.

There was no chance to speak to him as he led her through the thronging festival-goers. No chance until they came out into a side street where the people were less tightly packed.

'What's wrong with Mark?' insisted Belinda. 'Where is he?'

'Don't ask questions.' Joe Sharpe pulled Belinda up close, his wiry arm closing round her shoulders. She felt something press against her side. She glanced down and saw the cold grey glint of a knife. 'Don't speak and you won't be hurt,' he said.

Belinda stopped resisting as he walked her along the road.

171

'Where are you taking me?' she asked.

'We're going to your house,' said Joe Sharpe. 'Your friend's already there.'

'What do you mean?' asked Belinda. 'What friend?'

Joe Sharpe didn't reply.

They turned a corner and his grip tightened on her. 'One stupid move,' he growled, 'and you'll regret it.'

They stopped beside a parked car and he felt in his pocket.

Belinda's heart gave a leap. Cycling along the road towards them, his camera bouncing against his chest, was Kurt. He brought his feet down and came to a skidding halt on the other side of the car.

'Hello, Belinda. What are you up to?'

Belinda opened her mouth to reply. But Joe Sharpe was too quick for her.

'Her mother's had an accident,' he said. 'I'm taking her to the hospital.'

'Oh.' Kurt's face registered dismay. 'Is it serious?'

Belinda felt the knife blade at her side.

'No, it's OK, Jack,' she said. 'But could you tell Miss Adams where I've gone?'

Kurt gave her a blank look. 'Tell *who*?'

Joe Sharpe pulled the passenger door open and pressed his hand down on Belinda's shoulder, pushing her into the car. She lost grip of her balloon on a stick and it fell to the pavement.

'It's nothing serious,' Joe Sharpe said to Kurt, moving round the car and opening the door. 'You just carry on about your business. I'll see that Belinda's OK.'

There was a folded map on the passenger seat. Belinda pulled it out from under her. It was open to a page that showed an area of Willow Dale. She only had seconds before Joe Sharpe got into the car. She dug her hand into her pocket and drew out Miss Baker's lipstick, smearing a red circle round the street where she lived, then tucking the map down by her side.

Kurt was bent double over his bike, staring in concernedly at her through the side window.

"Bye, Jack,' she called as Joe Sharpe slammed the door and started the car.

Kurt wheeled his bike out of the way as the car reversed and then sped forwards along the road.

Belinda made a sudden lunge for the door, jerking it a few inches open before Joe Sharpe's arm came crashing across her to slam it shut again.

'Try that again and you won't know what's hit you,' snarled Joe Sharpe. 'Understand?'

Belinda slumped back in her seat, glaring at him. In the split-second that the door had been open, she had dropped the map out on to the road.

Her hope now was that Kurt had realised there

173

was something very wrong, that it was nothing to do with her mother, and that he would do something about it.

Holly came to the corner. She saw Kurt standing astride his bike, twisting round to watch the speeding car.

She ran up to him.

'Why didn't you stop them?' she panted. 'Where's he taking her?'

Kurt gave her a baffled look. 'He said her mother's had an accident,' said Kurt. 'But she called me Jack. Is this some sort of practical joke you've cooked up between you?'

'A joke!' exclaimed Holly. 'It's no *joke*, Kurt. I think she's been kidnapped. Did you get any idea where he's taking her?'

'Something fell out of the car,' said Kurt. 'Wait there a second.'

He cycled along the road and bent over to pick up the fallen map. Holly ran after him.

She saw the lipstick smear. 'That's the street where she lives,' said Holly. 'That must be where they're going. Kurt, we've got to get the police, quickly! I think they've already got Tracy.'

'Are you sure this isn't a joke?' asked Kurt. 'Tracy's on the float, isn't she?'

'No. She isn't. It's not her. I think it's Mark's mother,' Holly said breathlessly. 'Give me your bike. I'll follow them.' She wrested the handlebars out of Kurt's hands, knocking him off balance.

'Holly! Will you . . . *ow!*' He fell into the road.

There was no time to explain. Holly jumped on to his bike and was pedalling away before he could even get to his feet.

'Call the police,' she shouted back. 'Belinda's house! *Now!*'

There was no time to plan as she pumped her legs up and down on the pedals. No chance to ask herself what she could hope to do by following Belinda. All she knew, as the bicycle whizzed along the road, was that Belinda was in danger.

But what were they intending to do to her?

Holly's thoughts whirled away from her as she pistoned her legs and the bicycle shot like an arrow towards the long, gruelling hill that led to Belinda's house.

But Holly hadn't lost all caution in her mad flight. She knew she couldn't go crashing in there like the Fifth Cavalry. A dozen or so metres from Belinda's house she brought the bicycle bouncing up on to the pavement and came to a breathless halt.

She leaned over the handlebars, gulping in air like a stranded fish. Her legs felt like jelly. She leaned the bicycle against a hedge and walked slowly towards the brick gateway that led to the broad gravel drive at the front of Belinda's house.

She ducked out of sight. There was a car in the drive. And there was someone sitting at the wheel.

Holly took several long, deep breaths, calming herself down, and cautiously tilted her head round the brick pillar.

It was Mark in the car.

She glanced around. The long sloping street was utterly deserted. Everyone was at the festival. And the was no way of getting to the front door with Mark sitting there keeping guard.

Holly backed away and ran to the entrance of the next house along. She rang the bell, hearing the ding-dong sound echo in the silence. Agonising moments passed. No one was coming.

She ran to the side of the big detached house. The side gate was unlocked. She pushed it open and ran alongside the tall wooden fence that divided one garden from the next.

Holly pulled the camcorder round to balance against her stomach, and jumped at the fence, hauling herself to the top.

She landed lightly in the Hayeses' garden and ran round to the back of the house. The back doors were locked, but she had expected that. She had another idea.

She ran up the broad steps to the French windows, peering through into the long, empty room where they had sat and watched the Great

176

Mysterioso perform his magic tricks at the party.

A sheet of plywood was nailed over the pane of glass that had been broken by the burglar. Holly dragged a large earthenware plant pot over to the doors and balanced on the rim, clawing at the plywood with her nails.

It was hopeless. She needed something to prise the plywood off with. She looked round. Some old garden tools lay nearby. She grabbed a rusty old trowel and jammed it between the plywood and the window-frame.

There was a creak of nails. Holly put all her strength into it and the plywood suddenly broke free. She felt through the hold and yanked the bolt down. She crept in and tiptoed across the room to the door.

Holly heard the sound of voices coming from a nearby room. She slid silently across the hall to a door that was half open.

Joe Sharpe sat with his back to her, straddling a chair, his arms across the back, one hand dangling a knife. Sitting in front of him on a couch, their hands and feet tied, were Tracy and Belinda.

'. . . I shouldn't worry about that,' she heard Joe Sharpe say. 'We'll get your friend as well. And then we'll have all three of you.'

Holly saw a flicker in Tracy's eye as her friend caught sight of her.

'You won't catch Holly,' said Tracy, looking Joe

Sharpe straight into the eyes. 'She's probably talking to the police at this very moment.'

Belinda had caught sight of Holly as well, but quickly looked away so as not to alert him to her presence.

'It's true,' said Belinda. 'As soon as she sees I'm missing, she'll realise what you're up to. We've been on to you for days.'

'I'd give myself up right now,' said Tracy. 'You, and him upstairs.'

Holly glanced up the stairs. Tracy's words were clearly meant to warn her that Joe Sharpe wasn't alone in the house.

'We'll see about that,' Joe Sharpe said evenly. 'Because I'm about to send Mark off to get your friend.' He swung his leg off the chair and stood up.

'What are you planning on doing with us?' said Belinda.

'You wouldn't want to know,' said Joe Sharpe. 'But I'll tell you one thing: we'll be a long way from here before you'll be in any state to blab to the police. If you're left in a state to blab at all.'

'You won't get away with this,' said Tracy.

Joe Sharpe laughed. It was a sound more chilling than any threat he could have uttered.

Holly glided back along the wall. As she heard his footsteps approaching, she made a soft-footed run for the stairs.

She was up the stairs and out of sight before he came out into the hallway.

The sounds of someone in Mrs Hayes's bedroom came clearly to her ears. Holly crept along the landing. The door was open, and she looked inside. Mr Greenaway was at a chest of drawers, pulling out the contents. There was already a terrible mess on the floor, clothes and other things scattered about as he searched.

There was no way she could tackle him alone, but maybe she could lock him in there before he realised what was happening.

Holly slid her hand round the door, hardly daring to breathe. One sound and she would be in deep trouble. She heard him growl as he flung the drawer to the floor and reached for another.

The cold, sharp edge of a key touched her questing fingertips. Stiff in the lock, it was difficult to pull out.

The camcorder swung on its strap and hit the door with a loud thud.

The key came loose in Holly's hand just as Mr Greenaway's head snapped round and his eyes met hers.

She slammed the door closed and turned the key in the lock, hearing his bellow of surprise and rage and he floundered across the room and crashed against the solid wood.

One down! Holly thought triumphantly.

She ran to the stairs. The front door was open and there was no sign of Joe Sharpe.

Holly had never moved so quickly in her life. Down the stairs and into the room where Belinda and Tracy were being held. She slammed the door behind her.

'Is there a key?' she gasped. 'Quickly!'

'No,' gasped Belinda. 'Use the chair!'

Holly pounced on the wooden chair Belinda had indicated and dragged it over to the door, jamming the back under the handle and giving it a good shove to fix it in place.

Belinda held her hands out and Holly fumbled at the cords that held her. Even as she felt the ropes loosen she heard a shout. Not from Joe Sharpe, but a shout that came from above them. From Mr Greenaway.

'Joe!' they heard. 'I'm locked in. Get back in here!'

Belinda's hands flew to the bonds round her feet as Holly worked on the ropes round Tracy's wrists.

They heard a crash against the door. The heels of the chair shifted as weight was applied. For an awful moment they thought the door would come bursting open. But the back legs of the chair dug firmly into the carpet as the door handle rattled and a heavy shoulder beat on the outside.

Tracy let out a gasp of relief. 'They can't get in!' she said.

'Yes, they can!' shrieked Belinda, her face white. Holly and Tracy spun to follow the line of her pointing finger. A second door stood half open, leading into the dining-room. 'They can get in through the other room!'

Even as they ran towards it they saw a looming shadow outside the door.

Joe Sharpe stood in the doorway, his face red, the vicious-looking knife poised in his hand.

They were trapped.

14 The key

'*Geronimo!!!*'

Holly was as much taken by surprise at that sudden wild yell as Joe Sharpe was.

One moment Tracy was staring into his ice-cold eyes, the next instant she had leaped forwards and snatched the door shut in his face. Literally *in* his face. Knocking him spinning backwards.

With a shrilling laugh, Belinda grabbed a chair and shoved it under the handle.

'Is there a phone?' shouted Tracy. 'We gotta phone for help.'

'It's in the hall,' said Belinda.

'Creeping Jemima!' Tracy stared around the room. 'What are we going to do, guys? We can't hold them off forever.'

'The window,' said Belinda. She gave the chair under the door handle a kick to make sure it was secure, then ran to the window, which looked out over the side of the house.

They heard a thunderous crash against the closed door.

'Belinda! What are you *doing*!' said Holly. Belinda was at the window, wrestling with the catch.

'It won't open,' she said. 'It's one of those locks that needs a key to get it open.'

'So get the key,' said Tracy.

'I don't know where it is!' shouted Belinda.

An ominous sound snapped their heads round. The chair was slowly yielding to pressure from outside, its feet rucking up the carpet as it edged forwards. A hand groped inwards.

Holly ran forwards and hit out with the camcorder. There was a shout of rage and pain and the hand withdrew.

'The police are coming!' yelled Holly. 'They'll be here any minute.'

Thud after thud sounded, rattling the door as it inched open. It would only be a matter of seconds now before there was a wide enough gap for the enraged Joe Sharpe to squeeze through. And then what would happen? Holly dreaded to think.

Her two friends ran over to her, their combined weight forcing the door closed again.

Belinda tugged at the chair, pulling it away from the door and turning the door handle open.

'Belinda, don't!' Not realising what her friend had in mind, Holly grabbed the chair.

The door flew open at a shoulder charge from Joe Sharpe. He came crashing off-balance into the room, taken completely by surprise. Belinda swung the chair in a low arc, catching up hard against his legs and sending him sprawling on to the carpet.

'Got you!' Belinda yelled triumphantly. She jumped over the spread-eagled man and ran, Holly and Tracy only a split-second behind her. They tumbled together as they skidded on the polished wooden floor of the dining-room and raced through the door into the hall.

But their escape route through the front door was blocked. Mark stood on the threshold. As he realised what was happening he let out a shout and swung the door shut behind him.

They heard a crash from the other room and turned to see Joe Sharpe come staggering into the hall, his mouth twisted in an evil grimace, a deadly look in his eyes.

'Upstairs!' yelled Belinda.

They ran.

Holly felt Joe Sharpe's fingers brush the back of her jacket. She swung the camcorder blindly behind her and felt an impact. She didn't dare look round until they were at the top of the stairs. Joe Sharpe was clutching the banisters with one hand and holding his face with the other.

'Get them!' she heard him shout to Mark.

The three girls ran into Belinda's room. Along the landing they could hear Mr Greenaway shouting and hammering on the door.

Belinda heaved her bedroom door closed and

turned the key. The three girls stood panting in the chaos of Belinda's room.

'The rats!' said Belinda, gazing around at her things. 'They've been in here! The rats!'

'How can you tell?' said Tracy. 'It looks pretty much the same to me.'

'It's OK,' gasped Holly, trying to catch her breath. 'I told Kurt to get the police. But what do they want us for?'

'We were too close to having it all figured out,' said Tracy. 'They knew we'd set them up last night.'

'We know that,' said Holly. 'Jamie let slip to Mark that we were all staying here overnight.'

'So why didn't anyone tell *me* about this?' said Tracy. 'I wouldn't have let Mark pick me up this morning if I'd known.'

'We didn't find out until we got to school,' said Holly. 'We went to your house, but you'd already gone.'

'Didn't you realise I was *missing*?' said Tracy.

'There was someone on the float,' said Belinda. 'Someone pretending to be you.'

'It's Mary Greenaway,' said Holly. 'I'm sure it is. She must have sneaked into the school when no one was looking and put your costume on. They obviously didn't want Belinda and me to know you were missing until they'd picked us up as well. But what are they planning on doing with us?'

'They're going to clear this place out and then make a run for it,' said Tracy. 'I heard Mark's father saying something about Spain. They wanted the three of us safely out of the way so they could get a good start.'

'Greedy pigs,' said Belinda. 'If they'd just done a runner, they could have been miles away by now. But they had to do one last job, and now we've got them!'

Tracy stared at her. '*We've* got *them*?' she said. 'Are you sure about that?'

There was a thump on the door.

'Come out.' It was Joe Sharpe's voice. 'Come out and you won't be hurt.'

'Yeah, right!' shouted Tracy.

There was another frustrated bang on the door and they heard Mr Greenaway shouting to be let out of Belinda's mother's bedroom.

'What do we do now?' asked Belinda.

'Stay where we are,' said Holly. 'They can't get in here. All we need to do is wait until the police arrive.'

'Are you sure they can't get in?' asked Tracy.

As if in answer to her question, a series of sharp thuds sounded on the door. Not the thud of fists, but of some sharp object.

'They're trying to break in,' said Belinda.

'That fixes it,' said Tracy. 'We've got to get out of here.'

'Can we get out through the window?' asked Holly.

They looked out. The smooth green lawn of the garden seemed a long way down.

'What do you think?' said Tracy. 'Four metres? We could jump that easily.'

'Not on your life,' said Belinda.

'Oh, come on, it's not like I'm asking you to jump off the Empire State Building,' said Tracy. 'What do you say, Holly?'

'OK,' said Holly. 'Let's do it. You first.'

'I'll keep them talking,' said Belinda. 'You two get out. I'll be right behind you.' She ran to the door and hammered on it. 'Stop that!' she called. 'We're coming out.' She looked over her shoulder. Tracy had already got the window open and was hanging out over the sill.

'Geronimo!' she said and vanished.

Holly leaned out of the window. Tracy landed with a soft thud and rolled on to her back. She was up in a second, beckoning for Holly to follow.

'Are you coming out?' It was Mr Greenaway's voice this time.

'Yes,' shouted Belinda, piling things up against the door. 'The key's got stuck. Give me a second, will you?'

Holly swung her leg over the sill.

'Belinda? Come on,' she said.

'For heaven's sake, jump,' whispered Belinda.

187

Holly stretched herself to her full length and let go. She fell with a rush of air in her ears, her legs bent to absorb the impact.

The impact knocked the wind out of her for a few moments. Tracy grabbed her arm and hauled her to her feet.

They looked up at the window. Belinda's face stared down at them.

'Come on!' shouted Tracy.

'I can't,' said Belinda. 'I can't jump that far. You go and get help. I'll hold them off.' She vanished from the window.

'Idiot!' shouted Tracy.

'Come on,' said Holly. 'Let's do what she said. Get help.'

They ran round to the front of the house, hoping to flag a passing car or find some way of getting to a phone.

As they hit the gravel driveway, Tracy ran to the waiting car and wrenched the ignition key out.

'Just in case,' she said.

They came breathlessly out on to the pavement, and as they hesitated, wondering which way to run, the best sound they could have hoped for in the world came ringing in their ears.

Police sirens.

'Good old Kurt!' said Tracy.

Three police cars came blazing up the hill. Holly and Tracy waved for them to stop and seconds later they were surrounded by police officers.

'In there!' shouted Holly. 'They've got our friend!'

The policeman ran towards the house, their boots kicking up gravel in long spurts.

'Go get 'em!' said Tracy, her eyes shining.

Heavy feet pounded into the hallway. Holly and Tracy ran after them. Through the open doorway they could see a struggle going on up the stairs.

The fight was over very quickly. Mr Greenaway and Joe Sharpe were dragged down into the hall. Their arms were pulled behind them and handcuffs went on with a satisfying click.

'There's another one of them,' shouted Holly. Mark must have ducked out of sight when he heard the police sirens. But where was he?

Belinda appeared at the top of the stairs. 'He's gone round the back,' she called down. 'Quick! He'll get away!'

Tracy heard a sound behind her. She looked out through the front door and let out a yell. Mark Greenaway had come running round from the side of the house and was heading for the car.

He snatched open the door of the car and leaped in, his hand groping for the ignition key. A look of absolute shock came over his face as his fingers fell past thin air where the key should have been.

He looked round and saw half a dozen policemen

bearing down on him. He sat back in the driver's seat and stared blankly through the windscreen as he was surrounded.

The last thing he saw before they dragged him out was Tracy standing smiling on the steps that led up to the Hayeses' front door. Smiling and waving the key at him.

'Girls, you've got a visitor.' Tracy's mother opened the door and a smartly dressed woman came smiling into the room.

The three friends were in the long playroom in the nursery Mrs Foster ran. It was a few days after the eventful Saturday of the festival and the capture of the Greenaways. The excitement had led to a feeling of anticlimax for the girls, and it had been Tracy's mother who had suggested something to keep them occupied.

A children's party at the nursery. Complete with magic show.

They had borrowed books from the library and some props from the local Amateur Dramatics Society, and at that moment they were deep in rehearsals. They had even managed to get their hands on a magic trunk similar to the one the Great Mysterioso had used.

They recognised the woman. She was the police inspector to whom they had all given statements after the capture of the Greenaways.

'I thought you'd like to know how things are progressing,' she said. 'As it was due to you that the gang was caught. It turns out that everything you three suspected was more or less true.

'We've been in touch with the police in London. The Greenaways did live in Kennington. Joe Sharpe is Mary Greenaway's brother. From what we've been told, they were working the same game down there. Either at magic shows or faith healing sessions they would make copies of people's keys, and pretty soon afterwards there would be burglaries. They moved up here because it was getting too hot for them down there.'

The inspector smiled. 'I imagine they thought they would be too smart for us.'

'That was Mark's problem all along,' said Holly. 'He was so sure he was more clever than us that he gave us all the clues we needed.'

'That's for sure,' said Tracy. 'If he hadn't started off by lying to us we wouldn't have gotten suspicious in the first place.'

'We?' said Belinda. 'What's all this *we*? He had you taken in.'

'Not really,' said Tracy. 'I was just stringing him along to see how far he would go.'

The inspector laughed at the expression on Belinda's face as she heard this.

'Mrs Foster tells me that you're going to give a magic show for the children,' said the inspector.

'That's right,' said Holly with a smile. 'But we won't be asking them for their keys or anything like that.'

'I should hope not,' said the inspector.

'Would you like to see one of the tricks?' said Belinda. 'It'll only take a minute. It's going to be the grand finale, just like in the Great Mysterioso's show.' She walked over to the magic trunk and opened the lid. 'It's a special vanishing trick,' she said. 'Come on, Tracy. In you get.'

'Are you guys sure you've remembered it right?' said Tracy.

'Of course,' said Holly.

Tracy folded herself into the trunk and Belinda brought the lid down on her. She sat down heavily on it.

'Hocus pocus, never fear, let Tracy Foster disappear,' she said.

There was a knocking from inside the trunk and Tracy's muffled voice. 'You've forgotten to unlatch the secret panel.'

'That's right. You're not getting out of there until you admit you were wrong about Mark Greenaway,' said Belinda. 'Until you admit it was Holly and me who worked it all out.'

There was a frantic hammering in the trunk. 'Hey, you guys, come on. Let me out.'

Holly joined Belinda on the trunk. The inspector laughed.

'I can see I'd better leave you to do some more practising,' she said.

'Help!' came Tracy's voice.

Mrs Foster and the inspector left them to it.

'Hey! Guys! Friends! Peace!' shouted Tracy. 'OK, I admit it. I was wrong about him all along. Let me out now, huh?'

Belinda and Holly looked at each other and laughed.

'Have you learned your lesson?' said Holly.

'Yes. Sure,' called Tracy. 'I'll never disbelieve you guys again. I promise.'

They got off the trunk and opened the lid. Tracy sat up, grinning.

'But you've got to admit,' she said. 'You couldn't have done it without me. It was the three of us, wasn't it? In the end.'

'Sit on her again!' said Belinda.

The three friends laughed as they tussled. But Holly knew that Tracy was right. It was all three of them, the Mystery Club working together, that had come through in the end.

MISSING!

by Fiona Kelly

Holly, Belinda and Tracy are back in the sixth
exciting adventure in the Mystery Club series,
published by Knight Books.

Here is the first chapter . . .

1 *A change of plan*

'But I just can't manage!'

The Mystery Club heard Mrs Foster break off, sigh and continue listening to the voice at the other end of the telephone.

'Judy will have to get the train by herself, I'm afraid. There's no way I can get down to London at such short notice.'

The determined voice squawked again.

'Yes, I know she's a capable girl. So long as you're quite happy with that arrangement.'

Tracy turned to her friends, Holly Adams and Belinda Hayes. 'My aunt,' she said ruefully.

The three members of the Mystery Club were all together in the sitting-room, eating biscuits and listening with interest to the long-distance telephone conversation between Tracy's mother and Tracy's American aunt.

The voice on the other end of the telephone chattered again.

'If you'll just confirm the times . . . Yes . . . Yes, all right, Merrilyn, I suppose it would be more reasonable for me to find out from this end. I'll call you back.'

Mrs Foster slammed down the receiver and said crossly, 'Would you believe it! Merrilyn has changed her plans *again*. Judy is coming tomorrow instead of at the weekend.'

'Calm down, Mom,' said Tracy.

'It's just typical of your Aunt Merrilyn,' Mrs Foster began, exasperated. 'If only I'd had a bit more *notice*.'

'You can't go down to London to meet her?' guessed Holly. 'No problem. It's half-term, so *we'll* go down instead.'

'No,' Mrs Foster said firmly.' There's no reason why Judy shouldn't travel by herself to York. However, you could go to York and meet her there.

'No problem,' declared Holly. 'We'll meet her in York and bring her back to Willow Dale on the local train.'

'Right,' said Tracy in a businesslike way. 'Judy's plane lands at six fifty-five in the morning. It will take a couple of hours to get to King's Cross from Heathrow once she's picked up her baggage, so she could get a train to York about nine o'clock. I think I've got the current train timetable.'

'Do you ever *not* have a current timetable?' Holly said with a laugh. 'What else do you keep in that filing cabinet of yours?'

'Everything except her school work,' said Mrs Foster with some feeling.

Tracy laughed. 'Go and do what you have to do, and leave everything else to us. You don't have to worry about a thing.' She turned back to her friends. 'It's going to be wonderful having Judy here. She was my best friend, you know, when we were young. We used to do everything together.'

'Tell us more,' said Holly, settling herself more comfortably into the armchair, ready to listen intently.

'She's about my age,' began Tracy. 'We were born in California, just streets away from each other. We were brought up practically as sisters, until Uncle Jason and Aunt Merrilyn moved over to New York. Uncle Jason runs a company which makes costume jewellery,' she explained. 'It's called Scheherazade. They sell to the big New York and Paris fashion houses. It's really big money nowadays. Nobody wants to drip with real diamonds and rubies any more, not in the fashion world.'

'I can't see the point of all that jewellery anyway,' said Belinda. 'I'd feel a fool all dolled up like a Christmas tree.' As usual, Belinda was wearing a pair of old jeans and her favourite faded green sweat-shirt.

'I really missed her when they moved to the East Coast,' continued Tracy. 'We wrote of course, and called each other, but it's not the same.' 'The last time she wrote they'd just finished their new collection, inspired by this fantastically ornate jewellery from Thailand. I think Uncle Jason actually borrowed some of the royal jewels to give them ideas for the designs. Judy says that Beaumont, the big fashion house in Paris, was really interested in them.'

'Perhaps we'll be famous, just knowing her!' said Holly.

'It's not all fun,' Tracy told her. 'There was another thing Judy said – my uncle's sure someone is stealing their designs. You know, turning out similar designs and selling them to the big fashion houses before his are perfected. It's happened too often for it to be a coincidence, she says. My uncle's real worried about it. It looks like it could be someone in the company, so everybody's being suspicious of everyone else.'

'A real mystery!' began Holly with a gleam in her eye. But Belinda interrupted.

'Hey, I've got an idea!' she cried. 'You know my mother's charity parties? How about getting Judy to come and talk at one of them about her father's business? Mum's got a big do planned for next Saturday, and you know what they're like. She always invites local business people along.' Belinda grinned. 'They're the ones with the money. She's bound to have invited some jewellers. There's at least three or four jewellers' shops in town. They'll probably all be there. My mother's collecting for one of the children's charities. It might spur them on to pledge even more money if they know there's going to be a representative of a really famous American jewellers there.'

'Judy's not exactly a representative of Scheherazade,' said Tracy. 'And she's hardly going to give away the secrets of my uncle's new designs – not with Beaumont of Paris ready to buy them. She'd be crazy to tell rival jewellers what they're up to. New designs like that are worth a fortune.'

'But you said it's only costume jewellery,' said Belinda.' It can't be worth *that* much, surely.'

Tracy gave Belinda a smile. 'You obviously don't know much about the jewellery business,' she said.

'And you do, I suppose?' said Belinda.

'I know that a new design from Scheherazade is worth a lot of money,' said Tracy. 'And I know Judy wouldn't tell anyone about them. My cousin's like a clam if she doesn't want you to know anything.'

'The people at the party won't know that,' said Belinda with a grin. 'So I can ask her, can I? Do you think Judy would be willing to make a little speech?'

'I'll ask,' said Tracy. 'Do I get to come as well?'

'Of course! I can't stand being at my mother's parties on my own. I'll get Mum to send you each an invitation.'

'Great – it sounds like fun!' declared Holly.

'You must be joking!' Belinda exclaimed with a shudder. 'Tell us more about Judy, Tracy. Anything to get my mind off my mother's awful party.'

'Well – she's pretty, she's clever, she's good at athletics and tennis, she's got really good ideas for things to do – she used to tell me brilliant stories before we went to bed . . .'

'She sounds horribly like you,' said Belinda. 'No wonder you got on so well with her.'

'How long is it since you've seen her?' said Holly. 'She's probably changed a lot since you last met her.

'I get photographs, and she writes, like I said,' said Tracy. But I haven't actually seen her in almost five years, not since she moved to New York.' A note of sadness crept into Tracy's voice.

Holly tactfully changed the subject. 'What I want to know is,' she said, 'why have your uncle and aunt gone away without leaving any address? That sounds pretty strange to me.'

'My parents' friends do that sort of thing all the time,' said Belinda. 'When you live in the public eye all year you want to get away from the press and creditors.'

'You think they owe money?' Holly said, her eyes gleaming.

'No!' said Belinda. 'Holly, you just can't resist making a mystery out of everything, can you? It's perfectly normal and reasonable.'

'Well,' said Holly. 'Perhaps there is a mystery here, I wouldn't mind having a go at figuring out who's stealing Tracy's uncle's designs.'

'Now that's a mystery!' Belinda exclaimed. 'Maybe we can even solve it before Judy arrives!'

'We'd better get organised on it now, then,' said Tracy. 'We've only got hours before she gets here.'

Holly laughed. 'And we'd really need to go to America if we're going to investigate properly. I don't suppose you've got the times of aeroplanes to New York in that filing cabinet of yours, Tracy?'

'I'm afraid not,' said Tracy. 'Still, it was a nice idea.'

'Oh, well,' said Holly. 'Back to the drawing board. Maybe you can use your organising genius to make sure we're in York at the right time to meet your cousin.'

'Good idea,' said Tracy. She ran upstairs to find the train timetable from her bedroom. As soon as the three friends had made certain that they had the times of the trains from London to York worked out, Tracy phoned her cousin and relayed times and connections to her.

'More changes,' said Tracy when she came back from the telephone. 'She's travelling with one of my uncle's staff – a man called Tony Meyer. He's got business in London, apparently. Not that it makes any difference to us. We'll still meet her in York. I'm so excited. I don't know how I'm going to wait until tomorrow morning!'

Belinda and Holly exchanged a glance and smiled. Despite Belinda's wry comments, the two of them were looking forward to meeting Tracy's American cousin almost as much as Tracy was!

It seemed no time at all before they were standing by the barrier at York station, waiting for the London train to arrive. Tracy was still hyped up with excitement, jumping up and down like a nine year old.

They were too early, of course. Tracy had seen to that. They had taken a train from Willow Dale half an hour earlier than they needed, just in case Judy had found her luggage at lightning speed and been lucky with tube and train connections. The girls wandered round the kiosks along the platform, with Tracy talking non-stop, telling them about how well dressed and intelligent her cousin was until even Holly began to wonder if *anyone* could be that wonderful.

'The train's coming,' shouted Tracy. 'Come on!' She grabbed an arm of each friend and hustled them to the platform. 'If we stand on each side of the barrier then we can't possibly miss her.'

There was no point protesting that they had never seen the fabled Judy in their lives. Tracy simply told them to look for a five foot four American with blonde hair and enough baggage to stock a supermarket.

People streamed off the platform. It seemed as if the whole world was coming to York for the afternoon. They all surged through the barrier, one by one, two by two, group by group, until the platform was completely empty but for a solitary guard, checking the carriages to see that everyone had got off the train.

But there was no sign of a blonde American, height five foot four, with enough baggage to stock a supermarket.

Where was Judy?

THE MYSTERY CLUB

The Mystery Club members Holly, Tracy and Belinda love adventure and suspense. What better way to follow their exploits than to wear their specially designed T-shirt and record all your secrets in the Mystery Club notebook with a Mystery Club pen? Whilst reading their latest adventure you can make sure you're not disturbed with the unique door hanger. And don't lose your place with the Mystery Club bookmark.

TO OBTAIN YOUR KIT ALL YOU HAVE TO DO IS:-

1 Fill out the form below with your name, address and the number of kits you require.
2 Make out a postal order or cheque to Hodder & Stoughton Ltd for £4.99 per kit or fill in the credit card details on the form.
3 Send the form with your payment to The Mystery Club Room, 47 Bedford Square, London WC1B 3DP.

- -

Don't Miss Out – Be A Part Of The Action!

Sorry, only available to UK addresses until 31 December 1994.
Allow 28 days for delivery. Available only while stocks last.

No. of kits required at £4.99 each . . . .

Cheque or postal order enclosed to the value of £ . . . . OR

Card Number . . . .

Amount . . . . Expiry Date . . . .

Signed . . . .

Cardholder's name and address (if different from below)

Name . . . .

Address . . . .

. . . . Postcode . . . .

PLEASE SEND MY KIT(S) TO (please print your name and address clearly)

Name . . . .

Address . . . .

. . . . Postcode . . . .

ISBN 0 340 60455 7